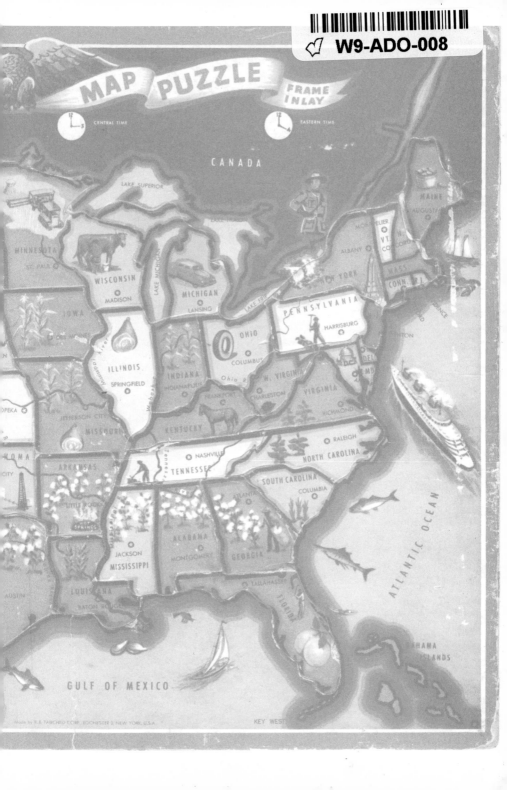

The English Major

Also by Jim Harrison

JIM HARRISON
The
English
Major

Grove Press
New York

9/08 24⁰⁰ B∩T

Printed in the United States of America

FIRST EDITION

ISBN-10: 0-8021-1863-1
ISBN-13: 978-0-8021-1863-9

Grove Press
an imprint of Grove/Atlantic, Inc.
841 Broadway
New York, NY 10003

Distributed by Publishers Group West

www.groveatlantic.com

08 09 10 11 12   10 9 8 7 6 5 4 3 2 1

To

Steve & Max.

Sons-in-law,

and friends.

"I write for the wish that comes true,
a terrifying concept."

—James Cain

MICHIGAN

It used to be Cliff and Vivian and now it isn't.

Doubtless everyone starts from somewhere. We were married thirty-eight years, slightly more than thirty-seven but less than the magic thirty-nine.

I just cooked my last breakfast here in the old farm-house, much changed during our marriage due to Vivian's whims and my labor.

I began to lose her during our fortieth high school reunion over in a park in Mullett Lake last year. Now I'm free, white, and sixty but I don't want to be free. I want Vivian back but it's been made clear to me that this is unlikely to happen.

At the reunion who would show up but Fred who left in the tenth grade. His parents were a higher sort, summer people from Petoskey who brought Fred up from Chicago to begin the ninth grade with us small town and farm kids.

Fred had trouble in Chicago but he also had trouble up here so his parents pulled him halfway through tenth grade and sent him off to Culver Military Academy in Indiana where it is supposed that they straighten out young rascals from prosperous families.

So Fred shows up for our fortieth high school reunion in an Italian sports car I had never even heard the name of before though we all agreed it made a growling sound sort of like the lion I heard at the Grand Rapids Zoo years ago. Anyway, he gave Vivian a ride. They were sweet on each other in high school. They were gone for over an hour and everyone got nervous, especially me, though nobody said anything even though everyone was beered up from the keg. When they returned there were grass stains on Vivian's knees and I got the idea that Fred and Vivian might have closed the deal. The last thing I expected was that my fifty-eight-year-old wife would become wayward. At the time there was no opportunity to get jealous or heartsick what with having to harvest fifty acres of sour cherries and ten acres of sweets, all of which took about a month during which the Fred-Vivian die was cast.

We got married after I graduated from Michigan State and Vivian had two years there. I taught history and English at the high school we graduated from and after our son left home Vivian became a real estate saleswoman of farms, resorts, and cottages. I took over the farm when Vivian's dad died while fishing perch up in the Les Cheneaux Islands near Cedarville. This man was a big strong asshole and had gone to glory from a heart attack trying to carry a hundred pounds of perch fillets and ice from a cabin to the pickup. Soon after the funeral Vivian's mother, Vesper, took off to a place called Carefree, Arizona, and thus it was I became a farmer after eagerly escaping this family fate by going to college and becoming a schoolteacher.

The shoe dropped at deer camp in November up near Helmer in Luce County in the Upper Peninsula. The snow was too deep to hunt for long so by lunchtime we were all back at camp playing poker and suddenly the game stopped and my friends told me that Vivian was having a hot and heavy affair with Fred who had his family's place on Lake Michigan north of Petoskey.

I took to drink which had never been a big item in my life. I drank a lot between deer season and the following June pretty much quitting two weeks ago after I thought I ran over our dog Lola, a thirteen-year-old Lab-collie cross. I had been at Babe's apartment fiddling around which is upstairs from the diner where she works in town, the drawback being that the little apartment always smells like overused cooking oil and French fries which I never liked. Anyway when I got home Lola wasn't in the pump shed at the back of the house waiting for her biscuit. I found her in the weeds underneath the back of my brown Taurus. I would have seen her maybe but I hadn't cut the grass and weeds in the yard. I ran around the yard weeping over my dead dog, turned the headlights on and called my neighbor Dan and yelled, "Lola is dead," and then for some reason I threw myself over the fence into the cattle tank which was still full though I had sold the cattle in early May. Dan showed up a little later at first light with a thousand birds singing. He laughed because I was covered with green algae scum from the cattle tank and was shivering. It was a miracle I didn't catch a cold. Dan showed me how my tires had missed Lola and that she had died of old age with a half-chewed gopher in her mouth. Lola would eat anything from gophers to snakes to woodchucks to one of three piglets I once bought. That was the only time I punished her. If you want pork that tastes like the old days you have to raise your own. Dan and I grabbed two shovels and buried Lola out behind the barn. "You better pull yourself together," Dan said, tamping down the grave dirt with his boots.

Curiously my life began to turn upward from the moment I discovered that I hadn't run over Lola.

It was strange after deer season when I called Robert our son who flew the Michigan coop right after he graduated from Kalamazoo College which cost us an arm and a leg. Now he lives in San Francisco. When I told him that his mother had left me for another man I was surprised when he said, "I'm not surprised." Since boyhood when he got involved in summer theater over in Petoskey Robert has been all show business. I can't bring myself to get on a plane but Robert practically lives on them. He said, "You grew in different directions." Since Robert was young he had had this irritating habit of emphasizing every fifth word or so whether the word deserved it or not. "Dad, let's face it YOU never were in sync WITH mom. When she was worried ABOUT her big butt you'd ONLY say that there's nothing WRONG about a big butt. YOU were supposed to say, VIVIAN your butt is not so BIG." Robert travels the world looking for locations for movie companies. When we found out in his teens that Robert was gay Vivian said she'd rather

her son was gay than a farmer. That's Vivian for you. She was always adding fuel to the flame, or as Dad would say, pissing in the whiskey. Once I tried to detox the butt situation by saying that her butt was only big because her mother's butt was big. That didn't work.

So here I am packing up the old farmhouse which the new owner is going to tear down, or so Vivian says. The orchard will be leveled and only the barn will stay. Robert and I each get 10 percent of the sale price and Vivian and her mother split the 80. The two hundred acres went for a million bucks which to me was an inflated price because I never netted more than thirty from it as a farm. Dan, my vet friend, said that a hundred grand isn't much of a retirement but I said it has to be because that's what I got. He said you don't even have health insurance and I said that's true.

As I said my life took an upturn when I found out I hadn't run over Lola and I quit drinking so much. An even bigger item came about when I was sorting through an old trunk and found a jigsaw puzzle from my childhood. There were forty-eight pieces for the states and no state had the same colored puzzle piece. In the box there was also information about the state bird and the state flower. I came to know this puzzle all too well because I spent a lot of my young life taking care of my little brother Teddy who was a mongoloid, what they call now Down syndrome. Teddy loved this puzzle and we spent hours and hours doing it over and over.

I took the puzzle downstairs and put it on the kitchen table and popped a nonalcoholic beer since it was only noon. I tuned in my big Zenith Trans-Oceanic to a polka program

over across Lake Michigan in Milwaukee. Vivian was embarrassed by how much she loved old-time polka dancing.
We cut quite a figure at polka parties. She said that the billowy dresses women wore polka dancing covered her big
butt.

The puzzle on the yellow Formica table before me gave
me an idea. Way back when I taught over twenty-five years
ago I tried to use Thoreau's *Walden* in a senior lit class. I was
better at biology, especially botany, but this woeful group
of seventeen seniors at least made an attempt at Thoreau
because they could see that the writer excited me. "Why did
he want to be alone? I like to hang out," a girl said. Thoreau
had said something to the effect that a man didn't own a
farm, the farm "owned" him. This hit home because half the
kids were from farm families and their parents never got
away to see much of the United States let alone the world.
In my case I had been to New York City and Washington
D.C. on our high school senior trip. I had gone to Chicago
once with Vivian and our son Robert to see plays. They went
several times but I went once. And I had been a chaperone
and driver for a bunch of 4-H (Head, Heart, Health, and
Hands) kids going to a big meeting at the Minnesota State
Fair in Minneapolis. I looked out the kitchen window at my
old brown Taurus station wagon with two hundred and fifty
thousand miles on it and figured she had some life left in
her. I looked down at the forty-eight states and their varied
colors. Tears formed when I thought of my brother Teddy
who drowned at eleven when the family took the ferry from
Charlevoix over to Beaver Island. Teddy never learned to
swim well and when we went fishing in a rowboat on a lake

or down on the Manistee River Dad kept Teddy tethered to his belt with a long piece of leather rein from the draft horse harness. Otherwise Teddy would jump into any body of water. It didn't matter on our farm pond which was only waist deep. The crossing over to Beaver Island that day was real rough with two major August line squalls and a lot of people puking over the rails. Teddy jumped overboard and the rein broke. We lost him by the time the ferry got turned around in heavy seas. Dad got real drunk at the Shamrock on the island and said that Teddy died the death of a noble sailor.

I dried my tears and ran my fingers over the map puzzle. Three days later I was off after sending the auction shares by check to Robert in San Francisco and Vivian's mom in Carefree, Arizona, where she lives only three blocks from the radio pundit Paul Harvey. I dropped by Vivian's office in Boyne City and she was miffed that I didn't give her the auction money in cash. "Now I'll have to pay taxes on it, you goof," she said with mean eyes. Our wedding photo was no longer on her desk. I recalled that at Michigan State she had a crush on a basketball player and when he didn't respond she had let the goldfish in her room starve to death. Several years back there was a summer month of a blue moon which is when you have two full moons in the same month. I tried to get Vivian outside to take a look but nothing doing.

The farm no longer owned me and thus it was that I left our green valley where I had spent so many years. I skipped the auction for emotional reasons and went trout fishing on the Pigeon River with a doctor friend. He's the most unsuccessful doctor anyone knows. He can't get up in the morning because he drinks too much. He put me on Wellbutrin to calm me down and to be frank he also gave me lots of samples of Viagra and Levitra for my trip, plus the phone number of a "hot chick" in St. Paul, Minnesota. I always listened to *A Prairie Home Companion* but not Vivian who thinks it's corny. When I had supper at the diner last night Babe told me that Vivian is riding for a fall. She said that Fred is having an affair with Vivian to try to recapture his high school glory. This is a little hard for me to understand because I don't remember high school as being glorious.

In the long summer twilight I went out behind the barn to bid adieu to the grave of my beloved Lola. I built side seats on my old reconditioned Farmall tractor and on the new John Deere so Lola could ride along with me. I'm not going to say that she was the truest woman in my life. At dawn I decided to take the jigsaw puzzle of the United States and throw a piece out when I crossed the border into a new state. It would be nice to throw away Michigan for the time being. Dad said I would always be "high minded and low waged" from reading too much Ralph Waldo Emerson. Maybe he was right.

WISCONSIN

Wisconsin is known as the badger state, the state bird is the robin, the state motto is "Forward," and the state flower is the wood violet. That said, certain problems come to mind. Of course the first day out is a shakedown cruise. I had crossed the Mackinac Bridge, known far and wide as Mighty Mac for its massive splendor as an engineering feat, and was west of Engadine on Route 2 when I realized I had packed away my bird and wildflower books along with a bunch of other belongings in a storage unit. I would have to play it by ear whatever that might mean. I was mildly irritated that Wisconsin had the same state bird as Michigan and decided that when I entered Wisconsin over west of Iron Mountain I would refer to the Wisconsin robin as an orange breasted thrush. There's so much repetition in farm work that I couldn't accept the idea in state birds. The wildflowers in the untilled pastures west of Engadine were another matter

I'd have to let pass as a different latitude meant different flowers. Babe had given me a dozen of those disposable cameras and also some new duds as a going-away present. When I told her she couldn't afford these gifts she said she had been saving up the five hundred bucks she owed me and bought the cameras and clothes out of that. When I stopped for a whitefish sandwich brunch near Epoufette a gob of tartar sauce dripped on my new blue short-sleeve shirt and the waitress rubbed out the stain with a clean rag and soda water. Her hand rubbing my chest made my neck hair prickle.

When I got back in the car I thought that though this waitress was a plain Jane about fifty years old there was something sexy about her. She smelled like Ivory soap, hair spray, and French fries so it couldn't be her scent. I had heard about pheromones on NPR and read about them in the *Detroit Free Press*. I decided it was because her features reminded me of a girl a few miles down the road who used to babysit Robert now and then when he was a child. When she was a junior I had her in both my biology and American literature classes. She was too sharp-tongued to be popular with her classmates. Her parents had moved up from Mount Pleasant to live the life of the great north but got starved out after a few years like so many do. Now a teacher would have to be a piece of damp firewood not to feel something toward the girls in his classes. Once I took Vivian down to Cedar south of Traverse City for the Polka Fest and when we got home the girl was sunbathing in her bikini out near the sandbox where Robert was playing. Vivian was pissed off and hungover and took Robert into

the house. The girl gathered up her stuff on the back porch
and we got in the car so I could give her a ride home. The
car seat was too hot and she said "ouch" then got up on her
knees with her butt in the bikini aimed at my face and spread
out a shirt and jeans to protect her flesh from the hot seat.
Thirty years later her butt is still a vivid painting in my neurons. I guess that's another part of the life of the mind or
what President Jimmy Carter said at the time about lust in
his heart. I was upset when Vivian told me that this girl was
promiscuous with the boys who came up for the summer to
stay with their families in the fancy cottages on Lake
Charlevoix. I said "that's too bad" and Vivian, always the
cynic, said, "Maybe she just likes to fuck." Anyway, the
waitress reminded me of an older version of this girl and
that's why my worm turned when she was cleaning the tartar sauce off my new shirt.

I took a photo of the Wisconsin welcome sign on the far side
of the Menominee River west of Iron Mountain. On the
other side of the road there was a big liquor and beer super-
market so Michiganders could take advantage of lower
Wisconsin prices. I bought myself a pint of hooch I'd never
tasted before called George Dickel. Since I was working on
a clean slate why not try a new brand of liquor? I felt a pang
when I saw Vivian's favorite butterscotch schnapps on a
shelf. It seems to me we were fine until Robert left home
more than fifteen years ago, nearly twenty actually. I mean
we were just a married couple and fairly happy and worked
together on the farm but not a day after we took Robert to
the plane in Pellston, where the great labor leader Walter

Reuther's plane crashed, Vivian got a job as a receptionist
in a realtor's office, and then she became a sales person, and
finally a broker. She was a whirlwind in real estate and I
was proud of her but then the job gradually began to coarsen
her. For instance we used to have three bird feeders out the
kitchen window but after she took up the real estate profession she had no time to feed the birds. She'd trot out of
the house in the morning with her cup of coffee and I
wouldn't see her until dark. I'd have supper on the stove but
first she'd take a bath with a tumbler of butterscotch
schnapps on ice. She got bigger because she didn't have time
for regular meals but instead snacked on potato chips, Oreo
cookies, and Pepsi. You couldn't tell her anything. At one
time she'd read good books but after her job she only read
paperbacks about international intrigue. I never saw any of
the money she made and saved which was supposedly put
away for our retirement which she planned on being in
Hawaii. Since I couldn't get on a plane I wondered aloud
how I was to get to Hawaii and she said, "You'll figure it
out." We never talked about her money again after she refused to loan me the down payment on a John Deere tractor. I wanted to get this big snow blower attachment to
make money in the winter cleaning out driveways for cot-
tagers who came up to ski Boyne Mountain.

   As I said the Wisconsin motto said "Forward" which
is well enough because you can't exactly go backward.
Vivian was behind me, that's for sure. I didn't pay attention
over a year ago when she looked up from her Robert Ludlum
spy book and said, "You look so forgettable, you'd make a
good spy." Maybe life is only temporary measures. Up in

our green valley northwest of Boyne City I thought everything was glued together including the fate of nations. I only
worried about the weather and if the cherry buds in the
orchard would freeze in late May or early June. Now in one
year I had learned you couldn't keep the world together.
You can't keep anything like it already is so why try?

On impulse I turned south near Florence knowing that
if I kept on Route 2 I'd wind back into Michigan and a
hundred miles where the road was only a tunnel through
dense forest. I was hankering to see some of the central
Wisconsin farmland and the northern Wisconsin forestlands
were all too similar to Michigan's. This thought reminded
me of when I taught school and one September a duller student of which there were many told me that when he was
on a summer vacation drive with his parents he noted that
many of the states looked the same. I said that the land was
there before it was divided into states. He said, "I guess
maybe you're right." I asked him if he had owned a United
States jigsaw puzzle as a child and he grinned and said as if
a thirty-watt bulb had sparkled in his head, "That's the problem, by golly. In the puzzle the states next to each other are
a different color."

I reached dairy land by midafternoon and took photos
of some fine-looking Holsteins, also a single beef herd of
Herefords which you don't see much anymore due to a
genetic disease I read about in *Michigan Farmer* magazine.
Now your basic beef herds are mostly Angus like I owned.
Once when I crossed a ditch to take a photo about a dozen
Holsteins turned around and pointed their asses at me in a
feminine way. I'd never know why, I thought. I hoped to

reach Prairie du Chien by supper time. I did poorly in my
one term of French at Michigan State but I always knew
"*chien*" meant dog so when I looked at maps and saw Prairie du Chien I imagined a huge field with lots of dogs running this way and that. Of course this turned out not to be
true so I turned back north along the Mississippi toward
La Crosse because I had seen a photo in a history book of a
big hill in La Crosse where Methodist missionaries used to
stand and look west at their sorry destinies as converters of
Sioux Indians to the Christian faith. The thought of dogs
got me down in the dumps about Lola. In May she was a
great mushroom hunter and when she found a patch of
morels she'd howl and I'd come running. Vivian loved mushroom hunting before she took up real estate.

   I was suddenly struck by the fact that until Lola and
mushrooms came into my head I hadn't thought about
Vivian for a couple of hours. What a boon. Maybe after a
couple thousand miles she'd disappear from earth. Maybe
I'd drive to Hollywood and marry Hedy Lamarr though it
occurred to me she must be about ninety now if she were
still alive. My dad had a photo out in his tool shed of her
taking a bubble bath. The world is a wobbly place and so is
my mind. I had turned on Wisconsin NPR and then turned
it off again because I was up to my ass in Iraq. I was trying
to remember from history books if the Sauk Indians had
come up this far from what is now Iowa. As the landscape
unfolds it's all we have to offer and it's not even ours. We
were always an army of occupation. You know that if you
read history.

I stayed in La Crosse two days for the simple reason
that I didn't want to cover a state in a single day which would
mean my whole trip would only take fifty days when I was
planning on a year. I had intended to camp but a campsite
near a slough of the Mississippi about deafened me with
mosquitoes. I moved into a nice room at the Best Western
where I could see the river. "Treat yourself, Cliff," I said to
myself. It was too late for a full dinner so I had a hamburger
in the bar and a beer with a couple of shots of Dickel to calm
my giddy road nerves. The bar was pretty crowded with the
younger set and I recalled that my alcoholic doctor friend
had said that Wisconsin girls on the average are the biggest
in the United States due to readily available dairy products
plus fast food. He was on the money except for a trim lass
up on the stage singing a karaoke George Jones tune. It was
a tough song for me about a guy who can't stop loving this
woman until they put a wreath on his door which meant the
guy was deader than a doornail. All in all, though, I would
have picked the singer over Vivian. The singer wore one of
those popular bare midriff outfits and her tummy rippled.
Until I dated Babe after I got the bad news at deer camp I
had been faithful to Vivian for thirty-eight years though
when you're farming you're pretty short on the side of opportunities. Actually, to be honest I jumped the gun a few
months with Babe.

MINNESOTA

It was dawn and my heart soared when I crossed the Mississippi from Wisconsin into Minnesota, the gospel state, bird is the common loon, flower is the pink-and-white lady's slipper, and the motto, *"L'Etoile du Nord"* which means "The Star of the North," obviously from a time when our government wasn't anti-French. Down at Babe's diner they served "freedom fries" for a while but then everyone would forget and go back to ordering plain old French fries. Clark, the owner of the diner, also took Canadian bacon off the breakfast menu because the Canadians wouldn't help us out in Iraq. When I crossed the bridge I flipped the Wisconsin jigsaw piece out the window, colored red with small drawings of a block of cheese and a square of butter. The Minnesota piece was pale orange with a drawing in the southern part of the state of a quart of milk, and in the north a little sketch of lakes and trees.

Driving northwest on the river road my thinking got shaken up when I took a left on Route 14 and up the forested hill into farmland toward Rochester. The river was so beautiful it made my breath short and the farmland, well, was just good farmland. My mind made an abrupt jump to the idea that my dad was a river town and my mom was farmland. Let me explain as best I can which is none too good. Dad was a section hand on the Pennsylvania Railroad which runs up through the center of Michigan, you know, Reed City, Cadillac, Mancelona, Alba, and which years ago connected with the Soo Line in the Upper Peninsula by train ferry crossing the straits. Dad was usually gone all week and just home on weekends and sometimes only Saturday afternoons up until Sunday later afternoon when he'd drive back to Mancelona where the section crew centered. Dad wasn't too polished to put it lightly. Mother said this was because he was brought up mostly by his father, his mother having died when he was eight. He was raised on the edge of the Mackinaw State Forest west of Pellston where his dad was a logger and trapper. I only have the dimmest memory of my grandpa who finally moved way up to Chapleau in Ontario and died there soon after. Grandpa lived in a little run-down bungalow and his Indian hired hand lived in a shack next to the house. The Indian never said anything because his throat and mouth got injured in World War II though dad said he talked a fair amount before the war. So Mother said Dad was rough in the corners due to his upbringing. She nicknamed him Fibber after the old radio program *Fibber McGee and Molly* because Dad couldn't say anything straight or plain. Everything in his talking was

humor and contradiction. He didn't drink during the week,
or so he said, but he'd have a few on Saturdays. He just
couldn't say a plain sentence. He wouldn't say his foreman
was a bad guy, his foreman was "a sack of maggots." We
had forty acres of bad, sandy soil he mostly pretended to
farm on weekends; fruit trees (plums, peaches, apples, sweet
cherries), chickens, never more than three cows, two draft
horses, a few pigs each year, and a half dozen acres of thin
alfalfa. I was thirteen when Teddy drowned at age eleven.
After that Mom worked cleaning a mansion in Lake
Charlevoix owned by real rich furniture people from Grand
Rapids. Not much time passed before she was managing the
other five servants plus organizing dinner parties and that sort
of thing. I never saw the inside of their house past the kitchen
where my mother had her little office in the corner. They were
old-fashioned formal people so that when I painted their dock
Mom made me wear a white canvas painter's suit. Anyway,
as my high school years went by Mom became more refined
and Dad seemed to go the other way until we thought he
might very well be becoming goofy. I suppose she had to go
her own way to survive being married to him. He'd call her
WB, short for "wet blanket." He was sixty-one and I was a
freshman at Michigan State when he fell out of the tree house,
a fine one he'd built for Teddy and me. The doctor said Dad
suffered a massive heart attack and was likely dead when he
hit the ground. When I was young Mom and Dad would take
Teddy and me to the saloon on Saturday afternoons and she
would drink beer, smoke cigarettes, and play euchre just like
the other country women, but then she became a lady. She'd

say to me, "You're lucky you take after me rather than your father. You'll make something out of yourself."

I suppose I did make something out of myself but after Vivian moved out some of my dad's characteristics seemed to emerge. For instance Mike at the saloon wondered why I laughed so much one grim early March night when a fresh blizzard had come down from Alberta. I had drawn up elaborate plans for a tree house even though I knew the farm had to be sold. I could always build the tree house up at the deer cabin in the U.P. of which I was one-eighth owner. I had been doing a lot of snowshoeing north of Harbor Springs and had built a pack sling for Lola for when she got tired of walking. I carried her like a papoose and she would lick the back of my neck in appreciation. I never used much garlic while cooking dinner for Vivian because she said she had her clients to think of but I had noticed old Lola liked garlic so I threw some in when I cooked three pieces of pork steak, one for Lola, careful not to burn the garlic because she didn't like it. With Vivian I had to cook all too many skinless, boneless chicken breasts to keep her ass in trim, but then late in the evening after I went to bed because out of farm habit I got up at 5:00 a.m. I could hear Vivian in the kitchen making popcorn. She would try to clean up the evidence but I called it the case of the disappearing butter. So I told Mike I was probably laughing a bit more because I was doing things differently than I had been for thirty-eight years and this caused a lightening of my mind.

❖   ❖   ❖

Driving north toward the Twin Cities after a poor breakfast (they short commercial chickens on feed and thus the
egg yolks are pale and flavorless) I began to get cold feet
about my date. I had called my doctor friend's "hot chick"
from the diner and she was angry that I woke her up though
the summer sun is high at 9:00 a.m. Her voice was shrill and
she said my doctor friend was a "weird asshole that tried to
get me to piss in his hat." I was dumbfounded by this information. She told me to meet her at eight that evening at a
certain restaurant and to bring a "fat wallet." It occurred to
me that she was maybe a professional lady, a woman of the
night as it were. Back in the car I checked the restaurant
out in my set of Mobil Guides that Vivian gave me as a going-
away present and it was noted that this restaurant was the
most expensive in Minneapolis. You could pick your own
lobster out of the tank and the wine list was "extensive." I
didn't even bring along a sport coat so I'd have to stop and
buy one despite my dislike of clothing stores where nifty
young salesmen look down their noses at hicks.

My cold feet got even colder when I reached a suburb
called Apple Valley where I didn't see any apple orchards
and the roads became crammed with cars. Some beeped at
me because I kept a little short of the speed limit. Vivian got
lots of speeding tickets but I've never received one in my
life. I couldn't understand the traffic because it was just
before ten but then figured a lot of folks must start work
late. I saw a pay phone near a liquor store and pulled off
(more beeps behind me) to cancel my date. On the glass
above the phone someone had written "fuck you jerk off"
in lipstick and when the hot chick answered she said "fuck

you" to my cancellation. I felt a little giddy with self-doubt
as if the world was telling me something I didn't want to
hear. I had talked to my son Robert a few days before and
he wanted me to get a cell phone so we could keep in touch.
This seemed odd as I'd go months without hearing from him
but I didn't say anything. Robert carries three cell phones.
He said it's the way the world works nowadays. I tried to
use Vivian's a couple of times but it seems my fingers have
been blunted by farm work and the numbers are so small
it's hard to hit the right ones. Her phone got to be a bone of
contention in our marriage because she wouldn't even turn
it off when we were romantic. Her point was why miss a
ten grand commission to fuck me for the five thousandth
time.

 Back in the car I started sweating because there didn't
seem a way to get back into the traffic flow for the time
being. I took a couple of photos of all the cars then studied
my road atlas. I suddenly had no intention of driving
through the Twin Cities though I had had a vague plan of
taking Interstate 94 up to Fergus Falls just because I liked
the name of the place. After Fergus Falls I had intended to
drop down to Morris to see an old student of mine by the
name of Marybelle who was married to a man who teaches
anthropology at a college in Morris. In my ten years of teaching I had only three students I truly wanted to keep in touch
with and Marybelle was number one. We had corresponded
every few months for the past twenty-five years about the
ups and downs of life. Marybelle could get as excited about
pistils and stamens as she was about the novels of the Brontë
sisters and the poetry of Walt Whitman. She was what you

call an off-brand peach, real pretty to some tastes but a little exotic to the local boys. I recall she wasn't invited to the prom. She was the only student from our school before or since to win a full National Merit and she went off to college at Sarah Lawrence in the east. She had arrived from Ann Arbor the last two years of high school I taught. Her dad headed some kind of government program for rural improvement but no one in our area much wanted to be improved so they stuck it out for only two years.

I was pleased that I chickened out on Minneapolis because Route 212 West was real pleasant. Minnesota became Minnesota. I drove off my main route onto gravel roads any number of times to take pictures of cows and wildflowers. I saw a bunch of bluebirds which were my favorite as a boy along with the loon that sparsely populates the north. For a 4-H project Dad helped me build fifty little bluebird houses and mount them on fence posts around the countryside. Once when we were after panfish on a small local lake and saw and heard a loon Dad upset me by saying that each loon contains the soul of a pretty girl who died young. I was in tears and he reassured me that they would prefer to live within a loon and fly south every year rather than grow up and marry some dumb farmer.

I checked into the motel and wondered what to wear for the picnic Marybelle had suggested. All of my what Vivian called "presentable clothes" scarcely filled a small suitcase. I spent a long time in the shower and laughed at my presumption that a fresh shower might be needed when I had had one at dawn in La Crosse. I hadn't seen Marybelle since early in September before she took off for college twenty-five years ago. We took a ride in the country and when I let her out she hugged me and said, "Cliff, you've meant so much to me." She had said in a letter that she never thought Vivian was worthy of my high mind. This wasn't a lot to go on to try to uncover a buried treasure.

NORTH DAKOTA

I drove across the state line into North Dakota with a glad heart and a feeling of romantic triumph with Marybelle at my side. She was going to ride with me to Bozeman, Montana, where a well-heeled cousin was going to give her a used car. When I had stopped in front of her house in what Vivian would call an LMC (lower middle class) neighborhood it was obvious that someone isn't attracted to academic life for reasons of greed. Only the sidewalk in front of the house which was a faded yellow stucco was in good shape. The yard was mostly mowed weeds and the screened porch was full of holes any dim-witted fly could find.

But Marybelle was Spring herself. She actually wore a soft cotton skirt I had been drawn to when she was a high school senior. She called the color a "pale bruised rose" and I was flattered that she remembered that I liked it that late May afternoon when we had graduation rehearsal, the kind that would lead up to a not-always-pleasant ceremony where you get in a donkey speaker who thinks he's auspicious giving an hour speech on how education is the "ticket to the future." Everyone is half asleep from a picnic of ham, potato salad, and deviled eggs. The auditorium is probably too warm and the seniors are sweating in their robes eager to get at their secret celebration which will involve beer, pot, perhaps meth, and certainly sex.

Back to the present. Marybelle swept out of the house like Scarlett O'Hara or someone like that. I'm not accustomed to women making a fuss over me. As luck would have it her husband was on a "dig" looking into an ancient buried culture up near Malta, Montana, along with their daughter who was a junior at Indiana University on full scholarship. This was where the husband got his PhD which some of my friends call the "fud" degree. Their son was in Namibia in Africa working with an environmental group called Round River, the name of which I liked because my dad always said that it would be nice if rivers were round which meant you could float them for trout and end up where you started.

I almost forgot! North Dakota is the flickertail state, the bird is the western meadowlark, the flower is the wild prairie rose, and the motto is a sort of wordy "Liberty and Union, Now and Forever, One and Inseparable." I gave Marybelle the privilege of tossing the pale orange Minnesota piece out into the Bois de Sioux River. There had been a big thunderstorm in the night and the river was high and muddy. We stood on the bridge and waved good-bye to the Minnesota piece bobbing south on the roiling current. Marybelle said she disliked the purple color of the North

Dakota piece and I said we'll have to live with it. I had only had a scant hour of sleep so somewhere along the way a nap was in the offing. I suddenly remembered my last nap using Lola as a pillow out in the cherry orchard in May when the trees were blooming. I could feel Lola's heart through the back of my head beating in what I remembered from college as iambic pentameter. All the local farmers were worried because the trees budded early which meant they were susceptible to a frost. Now for the first time in twenty-five years I didn't give a shit about weather what with the farm being sold. This was the fifth day that the weather had become meaningless and the concern for it had drifted from my mind, sometimes drifting back in but easily dismissed. Part of the mental slavery of farming is that you're always thinking it's too warm or too cold, too wet or too dry, or that a big wind is going to bruise the fruit.

Marybelle was curled up in the corner of the seat against the door snoozing which would have made me even tireder except I could see an expanse of thigh. I kept shaking my head because my perceptions were blurred at the edges from all of the wine we had drunk. You might say we had a humdinger night of love though she wouldn't take off her undies. "I can't take off my panties on our first date," she teased. After it happened I recalled reading Henry Miller in college where he said, "I came off like a whale." Even now in the car my prostate is thumping with a localized ache. I mused over the age difference of a sixty-year-old man and a woman of forty-three. It is what the sailing folk over in Charlevoix call a "far reach." Even though we were a mite drunk she embarrassed me at our lakeside picnic when she said that as a high school senior she had a fantasy of us screwing like dogs out in the hay field. It had an effect on me like touching an electric fence while standing in a puddle. She was sitting there on a blanket in a grove of trees by the lake sprinkling Tabasco on a chicken leg with her skirt hiked way up. I dropped my fried thigh and flopped forward, my head burrowing up her skirt like a gopher. It was salty lilac country. I was so hard you could have hung a pail of milk on my dick. It was twilight and we were alone but then unfortunately a carload of teenagers roared through the picnic grounds and a teenager yelled, "Throw her a fuck." Marybelle gave them the finger which was out of character, her physical movements in the throes of desire being quite elegant.

In between our bouts of love she had spoken distressingly of her marriage, in such questionable terms that it made me forget the recent dissolution of my own. Of course I had been tipped off in her occasional letters. Only last fall she had quoted an Edna St. Vincent Millay poem from our high school American lit anthology, "Life must go on, I forget just why." This had alarmed me but then the letter had come before I received the bad news at deer camp. I had walked out in the wintry landscape and watched big snowflakes softly gathering on pine boughs. Earlier during the poker game our alcoholic doctor friend had made a joke about something he had read in the *New York Times* to the effect that each vagina was as unique as each snowflake. We were all dumbfounded and then he said, "I'm here as a doctor to testify that this is not true. I mean there are billions of dicks and pussies in the world and there are lots of identical twins."

After breakfast at Wahpeton and before she fell asleep
Marybelle had said it would be nice to do some north and
south zigzagging on the way to Bozeman. I didn't say anything but this distressed me as I had intended to enter
and exit each state just once. She had even taken the U.S.
puzzle off the dashboard and laid it on the backseat none
too gently and Florida had fallen on the floor with its drawing of a NASA rocket heading into space. I settled down
after a while by thinking my plan had been too hidebound
and anyway I could resume it after I dropped her off in
Montana. I wasn't cultivating rows of corn or pruning fruit
trees or bailing alfalfa. I should be singing the song of the
open road.

She woke up near Jamestown after thrashing around
from a dream. She poured a cup of coffee from my thermos
and looked out at the landscape with suspicion. I turned
north toward Devil's Lake having read about all of the sub-
merged cropland in that area in *Farm Journal,* a nationwide
publication in which there is altogether too much information about soybeans, a crop not much grown up in my own
area. Suffice it to say that our farmers are threatened by the
bounteous Brazilian production of soybeans.

I was intrigued by the landscape and still half asleep,
the only thing keeping me awake was Marybelle's hellish
description of academic life which would stink a rat off a
gut wagon as dad used to say. Here it is in a thimble: her
assistant professor husband has ADD (attention deficit dis-
order) and can't finish his book which would spring them
out of Morris into a major university in the east or far west,
preferably someplace near the ocean. He's in a competitive

field as there are far too many PhD's in anthropology floating around the country tending bar, et cetera. She met him
in New York City when she was a sophomore at Sarah
Lawrence and he was graduating from Columbia and had a
fellowship to Indiana University, blah, blah, blah. Brad (his
name) was handsome and witty and she impulsively married him. Brad liked to think he was on the cutting edge of
everything including his idea of "pansexuality" which he
believed had a firm historical basis. Translated this means
he fucked his students. Meanwhile she had their two kids
but still managed to finish her BA in theater history. After
Brad finished his PhD they had moved three times to minor
colleges in Kansas and Missouri ending up in the compara-
tive paradise of Morris. They always moved by U-Haul
trailer and now the sight of one nauseated her. She nearly
divorced Brad when the kids were young because he gave
her herpes. They stayed together for the children. She had
been nearly bedridden for two years with a case of mono-
nucleosis. The reality of Brad not finishing his book had
thwarted their lives. The book was about possible Native
American cannibalism in prehistory (around Boyne City
the Native Americans call themselves Indians). All in all
Marybelle's tale of woe made farming or even real estate
appealing. I was this little fraction of her life that wouldn't
amount to much or so I decided.

Things turned up after I pulled off on a gravel road near
Fort Totten and I took a nap in back of the station wagon.
There was a nice breeze off Devil's Lake and I slept deep as
a stone for an hour. Marybelle had gone off for a stroll with
my binoculars and when I woke up she was fiddling with

my pecker finally sitting on it as if I were the seat of a chair. She said our second day was our second date so we could go "all the way," an old high school term. I heard a motor noise I recognized as a John Deere. Marybelle covered her face but I glanced out the side window and saw the farmer on the new model Deere, his eyes averted from us. I speculated that he was likely a Lutheran.

We headed over toward Rugby which is the geographical center of North America though there is nothing in the broad landscape to tip you off to this fact. Marybelle was miffed in a Rugby diner that I spent so much time talking to the German-Russian immigrant farmers who also seemed to have uniquely large heads. Back in the car she announced she had studied the map during my snooze and thought we should hit the Missouri over at Garrison Dam and follow it south sticking as close to the river as possible. This made me real glad she was along or such an idea wouldn't have occurred to me buried as I was in the idea of the multicolored jigsaw states. I was getting lightened up in my mind by the immensity of the landscape and the idea that moment by moment everything I saw was something I had never seen before. Marybelle had a tendency to babble about what she called "the arts." She read the *New York Times* on her computer and was real current on this world unknown to me. It reminded me of when I was a junior in college and thought I might be meant for big things though I didn't have a specific idea what they were. This was probably the genes of my goofy dad in me. Courting Vivian plus the influence of my iron mother brought me back to what they thought of as the practicalities. At the time Vivian pretended she was getting pressure from a lot of young men so I better "shit or get off the pot" as they say. We were short of money when we got married so on our honeymoon we only drove to Detroit to see a Tigers game and spend a night in a hotel called the Renaissance Center which didn't in the least remind me of the Renaissance I had seen on slides in an art history class. We had to get home in a hurry to help Vivian's dad harvest the cherry crop.

SOUTH DAKOTA

As we crossed the state line of South Dakota below Fort Yates Marybelle joked that I sounded like I had been in long-term parking for twenty-five years. My feelings were a little hurt and when we stopped to bury the North Dakota jigsaw piece under a rock in the austere landscape my mind wandered back forty years to when my brain was so alive I could barely sleep. Maybe my brain had developed three stomachs like a ruminating cow, thus radically slowing the thought process?

South Dakota is the Mount Rushmore state, the ring-necked pheasant is the bird, the flower the pasqueflower, and the motto "Under God the People Rule," none of which tells you much. What were these state fathers describing? I used to teach de Tocqueville to my bored seniors and there was a man with a silver tongue and pen. I was wondering if politicians had blurry thinking or they just couldn't write clearly about their thoughts.

My body was seizing up from sitting in the car so I told Marybelle I needed to take a walk for an hour every morning, something I did with Lola, rain or shine. A bit of the devil entered then because Marybelle wondered if I couldn't take my walks near a populated area so she could catch up on her cell phone. I made bold by saying that a populated area would defeat the purpose of a walk. These empty western areas are bad for cell phone reception so I said I'd try to park on a hill, and if that didn't work when we reached a good-sized town I'd park and go into a diner for coffee and a piece of pie and she could chatter to her heart's delight.

"I don't chatter," she said. "I exchange survival information with friends."

"What are you surviving?" I stupidly asked.

"Life itself. Marriage. Children. My stunted growth as a human."

"You seem real lively to me," I offered.

"You're seeing the best side. You draw out my best side. You were my favorite teacher. You mentored me."

I swerved a bit to miss a gopher who was eating a dead brother or sister squashed on the center line. It reminded me of a squirrelly student who wrote an essay, "Mutant Cannibals Ate My Mother's Body." This kid was utterly convinced of the world of aliens and flying saucers and was nicknamed Space Cadet. He was good-looking but all the girls thought him "weird." I heard that he nicknamed his dick "the force of one."

I was entranced by the town of Lemmon. Marybelle wasn't but I held my ground. I had an urge to live there just like there are certain paintings you want to inhabit say like Edward Hopper and Thomas Hart Benton. My head was riled because Marybelle seemed to become less like she originally presented herself in her letters or in our first hours together. I'm not saying she was deceitful but that she was slowly unwrapping herself and the fresh layers were as caustic as Drano. For instance, when we checked into the motel that afternoon in Lemmon it was pretty hot outside and she stripped down to her bra and panties and poured herself a water glass of Sapphire, a high-end gin I had bought for her in Bismarck. I was in the toilet again when I overheard her call her husband a "lamebrained motherfucker." My goodness, I thought, and on my way out there she was on her tummy poised to make another call when I left, her panties drawn up fetchingly in her butt crack. This was a fanny that could start a war and I felt blessed that I had the use of it for the time being, knowing how much I'd miss it when it was gone. An English poet said, "Kiss the joy as it flies." You bet I would.

When I returned I was sweating from a heavy load I had bought guessing that Marybelle might not be fit for dinner—a small portable Weber grill, charcoal, T-bone steaks, and salad. Through the screen door I heard her muffled voice saying something sexual in computer terms like "he really downloaded my hard drive." I felt a moment of pride but then it occurred to me she might be referring to another lover rather than myself. We men are scarcely unique. I started the charcoal before I went in, delighted that

she wasn't as drunk as I might have expected. Her hair was
wet from the shower and she was wearing brief lilac-colored
undies. My worm did a gentle flip-flop. She grinned broadly
and said it was too hot for full-blown sex and would I go
down on her a little to release her "spirit," a reasonable request. I dove off the high board with gusto realizing I had
dreaded my return to the motel after strolling the almost
mythological serenity of Lemmon. I had stood on the steps
of a large Catholic church after walking shaded streets and
heard angelic female voices in a rehearsing choir inside a
church. Now I was hearing Marybelle's not so angelic chir-
rups and yodels which were still somehow sanctified.

The grocery store plastic cutlery was unwieldy so we
ate our T-bones with our hands with bath towels on our laps.
I watched closely as a raindrop of pink juice trickled down
Marybelle's chest only to be absorbed by her bra.

After dinner including an acrid, bottled salad dressing
I had quite a head of steam under my belt and started making love from behind her but she fell asleep. I finished when
startled by her first slight snore. I recalled that once earlier
in our marriage Vivian and I had made love like dogs out in
the garden when she was wired on peppermint schnapps.
She said afterward that she "came" so hard it scared her but
she never consented to do it in the garden again. I admit I
wondered about this at the high school reunion when she
returned with Fred with grass stains on her knees. As they
used to say up home, "someone has been tupping my heifer."

Early morning and Marybelle was back on her cell
phone. I had a nice walk out past the edge of town and took
a photo of a fine thick-necked Angus bull who seemed to

be watching the meadowlarks fluttering around him. The owner stopped in his pickup and we talked farming in general and he was amazed at how many cattle I could feed on my sixty acres of alfalfa. Of course in Michigan we get so much moisture compared to South Dakota and some years I got three cuttings.

Our little conversation was so pleasant that I almost dreaded going back to the motel. Marybelle's husband had gotten a deal on the Internet and had given her three thousand minutes for her birthday. She talked to her "sister" in Minneapolis frequently and that got her cranked up on all available "issues." Of course the sex was beyond my fantasy daydreams but given more than enough sex you see that it isn't the be all and end all of human existence. In you go and out you go. I mean it's a fine thing but I had been hardly paying attention to the varying landscape that I had counted on lifting my spirits after losing Vivian. Instead I had become "pussy blind" as young men call it. My AD (alcoholic doctor) friend had said at a poker game that there was a certain kind of monkey that will give up lunch to see photos of female monkey butts. AD tends to say odd things when he's trying to pull a bluff during a poker game in order to throw the rest of us off.

Back at the motel I was relieved to see her studying the road atlas at the desk beneath the art print of the sad-eyed donkey wearing a garland of flowers. She announced with more than a trace of false humility that it would be nice if we could head south toward Norden east of Valentine, Nebraska, because it was a beautiful area she was familiar with as her husband had been on an anthropology "dig" in that area as a graduate student. They lived in a tent on the Niobrara River that summer and every day she bathed nude in the river even though she knew there was a nasty old professor jerking off in the bushes while he watched her. This didn't seem to be a very attractive story. I mean I don't think of myself as squeamish and I scarcely see human dignity at stake in sexual matters but I felt sorry for the old professor. He must have felt sort of silly when a session was over. Maybe he said, "Oops."

When Marybelle was taking her morning doze in the car I began to focus on her as a new kind of person. A few years back Vivian had sold two hippie couples a nice little farm down the road. Vivian said that they couldn't really be old-time hippies because they paid cash for the farm and one of the couples owned a brand-new Volvo. Vivian suspected that they had been in the dope trade down in East Lansing. Anyway, the two men liked to wear leather clothes and the women wore billowy peasant dresses and made a lot of baked goods which were none too good. One of the women, Deborah by name, told me she could tell I needed flax in my diet. Soon enough the men took to wearing bib overalls and they bought a tractor which they would drive around to no apparent purpose. They raised a hundred chickens for eggs and meat but they didn't have the heart to kill any for dinner. One of the women brought me some flaxseed bread that only Lola would eat if amply spread with butter. I caught a calf so she could pet it and she burst into tears at the beauty of the calf. None of them seemed to know anything in particular but were full of general good feelings. Vivian said they must be keeping their THC levels pretty high. One Sunday we went to a picnic of scorched chicken at their place. There were many of their friends up from downstate and most of the cars were pretty fancy. All of these people treated each other as if they were the most fascinating people on earth though I didn't hear anyone say anything of particular interest. They were that new kind of Democrat who didn't seem to know any working people. They were limited to their own breed. Late one fall with the usual hard winter coming the two couples moved to Maui in the Hawaiian Islands. They were disappointed when we wouldn't accept their old chickens or buy their tractor.

Marybelle was dozing with her feet up on the dashboard. The Taurus air conditioner was on the blink and with her legs up they caught the window breeze. Cliff, I said to myself, you be careful. This isn't Heidi or Mary Poppins sitting next to you. Marybelle had mentioned that she had phases when she was a tad "bipolar," one of those terms I had seen in the modern-living pages of the *Detroit Free Press* though it only made me think of the Arctic and the Antarctic. I wasn't too worried because she said she carried medications. Vivian had told me the year before our split up that if I developed some mental problems I might be a more interesting person. My mom used to say that Dad had mental problems but before she died she admitted that Dad just had too much life in him for one body.

NEBRASKA

There is the idea that I might dip Marybelle's cell phone in the toilet or a full sink while she's asleep. It has me fit to be tied. We spent a fine day driving south from Lemmon all the way to Nebraska with a specific kind of grandeur to the landscape, truly the Great Plains, a subtlety to rolling hills and rocky escarpments that doesn't suit people like Marybelle who want snowcapped postcard mountains. On the Standing Rock Indian Reservation I wandered off the main route and saw three Indian boys riding hell-bent bareback heading off cows near Thunder Butte. It was breathtaking, sort of an old-timey image of days gone by. This was a wonderful world without the eyesores of ski resorts or golf courses. When you've spent your lifetime teaching and farming up in northwest Michigan, a high-end summer and winter resort area, it can wear you out watching people have fun at top speed. Hardly anyone rows a boat anymore. It's

big motorboats in the summer and snowmobiles in the winter, the noise of which used to drive Lola daft, not to speak
of me.

Meanwhile rather than the landscape Marybelle was
staring at her cell phone to see if enough power for a signal
might arise. She finally picked up reception when we crossed
Interstate 80 near Kadoka and consequently had to sit there
for an hour. She could tell I was becoming irritated when I
walked off toward a diner to have a piece of midafternoon
pie and coffee. She claimed she has some "issues" to resolve
with her Minneapolis friend. At the diner I got to wondering about cell phones and also Vivian's e-mail binges with
her mother in Carefree, Arizona, and also our son Robert
in California with whom she daily exchanged whatever. I
was amazed to discover that they also could send photos
over the computer. Robert had sent one of himself and his
boyfriend from when they had gone to a party dressed up
as ostriches. This was the boy who liked to hoe the garden
with me and even enjoyed panfishing though I had to bait
his hook because he couldn't deal with earthworms. I was a
little irked because I had promised to call Robert who would
inevitably give me news of Vivian. My thoughts were interrupted by a comely waitress standing on a stool to fill an old-
time coffee urn. My dad had been on the bum out west for
a year right after World War II and told me that on the road
he had favored waitresses because he was always hungry
and waitresses smelled like beefsteak. He was part of our
armed forces that liberated Paris and he said when he got
back on our shores he hadn't eaten a good beefsteak in two
years. Ever after he was partial to beefsteak and could eat

two pounds of cheap round at a sitting. He also sprayed Tabasco on about everything except dessert and mother said this was because he chewed tobacco (Red Man) and needed the hot pepper bite to taste anything.

When I got back to the car I paused at the tailgate because Marybelle was still on the phone and heard something to the effect that perhaps she was orgasmic with me because she was subconsciously resolving issues with her father with whom she still had a ruinous relationship.

I thought this one over while feeling a twinge in my knees from our dawn workout. We woke early because we were both asleep by nine. Marybelle came out of the shower at first light in the lightest pale blue summer robe covered with tiny red roses. She pulled on fresh undies and her bare butt under that robe was akin to touching an electric fence. I murmured a question about how she kept in such fine shape and she answered "my Pilates tape." I barely had a sip of our motel coffee before she sent me off to the office to get a tape machine to hitch to the TV. The google-eyed night clerk joked that it was "a little early for porn" to which I didn't respond. Within minutes I was trying to keep up with Marybelle who was making violent movements in unison to a black man and a room full of ladies in Los Angeles. It was too fast for me and when I sat down Marybelle teased that she thought farmers were strong. I lifted her up on my shoulders and in the mirror the top half of her body was cut off and my stiff wanger was sticking out of my briefs. Her head tapped the ceiling light fixture and my chin took quite a pounding on the bed. When I took a shower I found myself humming the Christmas carol with the line "while shepherds watched their flocks by night"

and remembered the Christmas morning of his eighteenth
year when Robert told us he was gay but then we had already
guessed. There were tears and embraces.

I'm rarely pissed off but became so when we entered
Nebraska and took a look at the Niobrara River valley south
of Merriman. Nebraska appeared as a dreamland and I saw
a small farmstead near the river that made my mouth dry
and my heart begin to ache at the swindle I had experienced.
My mother-in-law always said that I was due 25 percent on
the eventual farm sale for working it all these years. How
precisely this became 10 percent I'll never know. My alcoholic doctor friend, AD, asked me if I had got it in writing
and I said no. I said that if you can't trust your wife, who
can you trust? In that he had had three wives and was courting a possible fourth he thought this was funny. When I
sounded sad on the phone Robert had offered me his 10 percent which I refused. He said that he and his "significant
other," sometimes called "lifetime partner" though there
have been a number of them, had just bought a condo
overlooking a place called the Presidio for more than a million bucks. I was stunned. I could imagine a farm being worth
that much but not an apartment stacked on top of other
apartments. My idea was to get a little retirement farm but I
couldn't do that on a grubstake of a hundred grand except
maybe in the Upper Peninsula where last deer season I had
looked at a forty-acre farm with a small house and barn for
forty grand. I mean I needed something leftover to live on.

When we reached Valentine and the Rain Motel (free
flyswatter) I called Robert who was busy on two other lines
so our confab was brief.

"Dad, Dad, Dad, DAD, Mom thinks Fred is CHEAT-ING on her and he already WANTS to borrow some MONEY."

I thought this was funny and said so and Robert said I was full of sour GRAPES. He said he had also sent his hundred grand back to my bank account because he had recently made a bundle. When I got off the phone Marybelle stood with her cell phone poised against her left tit and asked if I was sorry that my only child was gay. I said nope, everyone is who they are.

I forgot to say that I tossed the yellow South Dakota jigsaw piece off the bridge into the Niobrara. Nebraska is the Cornhusker state, the western meadowlark the state bird (the same as North Dakota!), goldenrod, considered a noxious weed in northern Michigan, is the flower, and the ordinary "Equality Before the Law" is the motto. Of course this was never quite true any place. Before we turned south in Martin, South Dakota, there was an ominous road sign for Wounded Knee. One year I tried to teach my seniors *Crazy Horse* by Mari Sandoz. Even the dullest, uneducable student can get cranked up about injustice. The hardest item was that there were two mixed-blood Chippewas (Anishinabe) in the class who were embarrassed about discussions of injustice toward Indians but even they laughed when our star quarterback bellowed at them, "You should have shot us when we got off the boat!"

I was sitting on the Taurus tailgate listening to the muffled chatter of Marybelle through the screen door of our motel room when I thought, "Fuck it, I'm going downtown" just as I had as a boy. I thought, "She does her thinking out

loud," about Marybelle, maybe a new development in our
culture just as twenty-five years ago when I quit teaching I
could see the onslaught of the new culture where everything
including education had to be fun or amusing.

Marybelle had had her Minneapolis friend look up a
food Web site which told us that in Valentine a place called
the Peppermill was the place to eat. I wrote out a note to
say where I'd be and stuck it in the door catching a glimpse
of Marybelle on the bed chattering with a hand on her crotch
itching or something else. During an antic moment in the
middle of the night I had said, "Fee, fi, fo, fum, who is sitting on my head?"

On the walk over to the Peppermill I speculated on how
much more of Marybelle I could take. A kind of free-floating
fatigue was setting in that recaptured my last year of teaching twenty-five years ago. It was a year from hell with a new
principal fresh out of Central Michigan University wearing
a PhD like a lei. She had a relentless smile but was mean as
an African bee. She was a virtual evangelist for the new
gospel that every young person is "creative" and immediately sensed that I was a nonbeliever. As a mediocre student
and teacher of literature I had seen no evidence of this creative streak in students. I nicknamed the woman Snog for
the peculiar snort at the end of her false laughter. The nick-
name got around and she was enraged when she heard of
it, accurately suspecting me. She was top heavy and walked
as if she were pumping a bicycle uphill. After she addressed
the PTA on human potential, parents began to think their
children might have a future beyond auto mechanics or
getting knocked up and married. These were the same moth-

ers who would say, "My Debbie doesn't have time to read a whole book." Anyway, when May rolled around I was so tired of teaching that my whole system went limp as a noodle and on the way to the Peppermill I had to speculate on what kind of exhaustion was in the offing with Marybelle. She placed a high value on what she called her "spontaneity" and I had pretty much spent a lifetime of going to bed at ten and getting up at 5:30 a.m. even in the winter when you had to wait two hours for daylight. Acrobatic sex is fine in the middle of the night but ever since Morris, Minnesota, the morning greeted me with a stiff neck and heavy limbs. My friend AD liked to joke about the frequency of heart attacks in older men having affairs with younger women but that didn't slow him down. I figured that in a few days after I dropped her off in Bozeman I'd rent a cabin beside a river and only sleep and fish for a week and not incidentally allow my sore dick to heal.

NEBRASKA II

Grave considerations took place during my first drink at the Peppermill. Large ranchers and bona fide cowboys surrounded me, their hat brims stained with sweat, but I was oblivious. It had become apparent that Nebraska deserved two chapters in my trip journal. This of course would vitiate my sense of symmetry but there was an idea that my rage for order came from being an orchard man. When you're raising cherry trees all of the trees are planted on a specific geometrical grid for efficiency in spraying weed killer and pesticides and for ease in picking. This infantile sense of order tended to infect my life at large. Up at 5:30 a.m., coffee, oatmeal, perhaps sausage (homemade), and fresh eggs giving one of the yolks to Lola. Listening to NPR and grieving more recently over the absence of Bob Edwards who was the sound of morning as surely as birds. Reading a paragraph or two of Emerson or Loren Eiseley to raise the level of my thinking. Going out to feed the cattle if it was during our six months of bad weather. If they were out in the pasture Lola and I would stand there counting to make sure none had slipped through the fence. Feed our few chickens and the couple of pigs we kept for meat. Bring Vivian coffee and a sweet roll or donut at eight. Listen to her sing "That's Amore" in the shower because she simply adored Dean Martin. "Boy, would I jump his bones," she once said. Pruning cherry trees, plowing, picking, spraying, fence repairs. Go to the IGA in Boyne City at 11:00 a.m. to pick up the mail (usually none) and the *Detroit Free Press* to read at lunch. A thirty-minute snooze in my La-Z-Boy chair.

It was unpleasant to think about this schedule. I ordered another drink and looked at the cowboys and ranchers around me and figured they doubtless had similar routines. There was an urge to imitate Marybelle's so-called spontaneity and plumb give Nebraska two chapters. Where was she anyway? In bed on the cell phone? And it was obvious that some states deserved short shrift. During a second-grade spelling bee I had spelled Rhode Island "Rode Island," the audience laughed and I fled the stage in tears, thus I felt mean minded about that state. Georgia was also on my shit list because of a girl from Columbus, Georgia, I had dated as a college sophomore while Vivian was busy starving her goldfish over the basketball player who ignored her. The Georgia girl was out of place at Michigan State but she got a free ride because her army officer father taught ROTC. She was obsessed with football. We met in the obligatory social science class, a course without an apparent subject matter, and within a week I was doing a lot of her schoolwork. She reminded me of an almost overripe peach and her soft mellifluous voice drove me batty though she wouldn't go beyond innocent petting. I mean I wasn't even allowed to suck her tits. I was enough of a horse trader to at least bargain for a look and when I wrote a midterm paper for her I was treated to a nude interpretive dance on the throw rug in my rented room. She flopped and writhed with vulgar abandon but it was hands off.

Our relationship ended when she was put on social probation after being caught overnighting in a wing of a dorm reserved for football players. I was dumbstruck with jealousy that she would freely give her ripeness to these louts while denying sensitive me who had recently gotten an A+ for my term paper on Wordsworth's *The Prelude*.

Where the hell was Marybelle? I called the motel from a pay phone and got nothing, then quit my brain work and began chatting with two ranchers about cattle prices and the effect of the mad cow embargo on Canadian beef. We went on to the squirrelly Japanese shutting us down and the rancher by the name of Orville said a big freighter headed for Japan had to dump two hundred million worth of beef in the Mindanao Deep, the deepest place in the Pacific, and it was said that ten thousand sharks surrounded the ship gobbling choice beef. Orville had been drinking pretty hard and doubt colored the faces of his listeners. These fellows reminded me of the old days, my father's generation, when stories were told slowly and savored. Nowadays with short attention spans everyone rushes for the punch line.

Suddenly there was a shriek and a sob and we all swiveled in our chairs. It was Marybelle with a deputy holding her elbow. She flung herself weeping into my arms in her too short summer skirt and sleeveless blouse. "I found you!" she shrieked.

The upshot was that she had wandered out of the motel without seeing my note. She was talking on the cell phone to her "sister" in Minneapolis and oblivious to her surroundings. She had walked a long ways out the north end of Valentine then doubled back toward the east and by the time she hung up she had no idea where she was and also had forgotten the name of our motel. A kind old lady weeding her flower bed had called the police and the cop eventually brought her to the Peppermill. With the courage offered by whiskey I had ordered a three-pound porterhouse which turned out to be the finest steak of my long life. To be frank I was thrilled. Marybelle had several gin drinks and made a sandwich out of a dinner roll and a pile of my steak fat.

"I've always loved steak fat. We can work it off later," she said with a lurid smirk. "There's something about Nebraska that has me sexually wired."

I thought this over dolefully. My porterhouse had a labial rose rareness and I thought about how things get confused with desire. Never had I felt so absent of sexual desire. It was likely time to fall back on the pill bottle of Viagra and Levitra AD had given me with the warning, "Take one of these suckers and you're in for a long haul." I didn't even want a short haul. Luckily I had some all-purpose steroid ointment in my Dopp kit that should work for my bruised member. Mom used to say that one of the worst things that could happen to a person was answered prayers. Farm work allowed lots of free time for sexual fantasies or "pussy trances" as AD called them. Vivian has subscribed to a movie rental company called Netflix and I had watched parts of many movies with her before my bedtime and in my mind's eye while working I had behaved shamefully with Ashley Judd and Penelope Cruz. Now that I had a woman on my hands nearly their equal I was ready to parachute her into darkest Africa. I noted while finishing my enormous porterhouse that when Marybelle flounced off to the toilet with an unnecessary and half-drunk wag to her ass the cowboys at the bar smirked then glanced at me with a mixture of envy and sympathy.

On the stroll home I began to think of our motel door as the gates of hell. Marybelle clung to me despite the hot evening then leaned against a streetlamp leering at me with the naked face of female lust while singing "Tura Lura Lural (That's an Irish lullaby)" for some reason. In our room toilet I felt sexless as a bowl of oatmeal and dropped one of my potency pills with a feeling that I was facing the gunfight at the OK Corral. In the middle of the night she barged into the toilet while I was applying the not-so-soothing ointment to my weenie. "Your dick is a mess," she sleepily whispered on the potty. I said that she had been in pretty close contact and she might have noticed before now and then I went back to bed in a huff.

When the stores opened in the morning I bought my first cell phone at Marybelle's insistence so if she got lost again I'd be able to retrieve her. I also bought a small tent and two light summer sleeping bags because Marybelle thought it might be nice to camp out on the Niobrara River near Norden, the scene of her anthropologist husband's graduate student dig during the first and only "golden" year of her marriage. Before we left town I leaned against the Taurus and called my son Robert in San Francisco.

"Dad, it's only seven in the morning for GOD'S SAKE." I apologized. I don't mean to present Robert as a nitwit. He has sent me many books on the human genome plus all of Timothy Ferris's books on astronomy. Robert always said that he had the soul of an artist and the mind of a scientist and that's why he ended up in the movie business. I must say that I wasn't able to follow the logic of the statement.

We found a pleasant, shaded campsite near the river and I set up the tent. Marybelle put on an actual teeny-weeny-polka-dot bikini which I regarded with no interest. While she sunned herself I walked down to the river, sat on the bank, and read yesterday's Lincoln (the state capital) newspaper. I make great effort to avoid thinking about politics. I think of myself as a Democrat but my party had been sorely disappointing in recent years while the Bush Republicans remind me of the mean-minded fraternity boys at Michigan State in the old days who were full of vicious pranks. It didn't help that I had once taught high school civics for a whole year in which one rehearses for the numb minded the ideals of our ideal government. It had occurred to me that elections tended to illustrate the abject failure of our sodden, fun educational system. Civics as a course offered high ideals that never seemed to present themselves.

A scream pierced the hot, late morning air. I came running. Not ten feet from where Marybelle, now topless, was sunning herself, a small rattlesnake lay irritably coiled. "Kill it!" she screamed. I pushed it away with a stick which it struck. "I thought you were green," I said.

We moved camp to a bare sandbar next to the river, inadvisable if it rained hard. Marybelle thought a swim might help my wounded member which I had said felt like it was boiling. The river was barely waist deep and I sat still facing the hopefully healing waters while Marybelle porpoised and flapped. She stood and looked around quizzically, then pointed out the thicket where the old masturbatory professor had spied upon her.

The rattlesnake had made camping impossible for Marybelle and I thought about my tiring wallet when I packed the gear for the trip back to the motel. Lucky for me she had a sunburn which meant I'd get to sleep an entire night.

WYOMING

It was my quiet prayer when we crossed the Wyoming border that a fresh state would make Marybelle's behavior less
antic. Without the exhaustion of sex my night had been
restless and I woke for good at 5:00 a.m. when I heard a
meadowlark out the motel room's back window. This lovely
clear trill was diminished when Marybelle in throes of a
dream wagged a hand in the air and growled the word
"fuck." The room smelled like our kitchen when my mom
canned pickles because I had dabbed vinegar on Marybelle's
sunburn which she claimed had helped. I had felt vaguely
like a doctor and her sweaty naked body had looked par-
ticularly mammalian with the location of her parts similar
to Lola's. My own wounds had subsided from outright pain
to a maddening itch which it would have been foolhardy to
scratch. I endured rather than prevailed. My senior students
had yawned when I tried to teach them the glories of

Faulkner's Nobel Prize speech. A chunky little cheerleader named Debbie who would later grow into a human bowling ball squeaked, "I don't get it."

Because of her sunburn Marybelle wore only one of my large-sized light cotton T-shirts. A gas station attendant in Chadron was treated to a sleeping beaver shot when he washed our windshield. He smirked and blushed highlighting his troubled skin. Marybelle had been sleeping a couple of hours since Valentine. I was puzzled a week into my trip which made me so philosophical that there was a lump beneath my breastbone. I wavered between being absorbed in the glories of the landscape (I took a number of photos of a group of Chianina bulls, an Italian breed) and thinking about three friends, really long term acquaintances who had passed on to the next world in the last year, or possibly to no world at all. It seems we are all only one medical test away from certain doom. The innocuous lump in his nose ended up eating his face. That sort of thing. My thinking had not been clarified by the first five states but then the devil herself was beside me on the seat snoring softly, curled against the door with the shirt pulled up revealing the fetching beastliness of her rear end. I was amazed at the graduality of the return of desire. Twenty-four hours without it and now it was beginning again like a tiny forest spring and soon enough I'd again be a butt-kissing dog despite my dysfunctional member.

West of Chadron I stopped at Fort Robinson to see the old U.S. cavalry remount station which once handled five thousand horses, but mostly to see the death site of the grand Lakota warrior Crazy Horse. I had read about him in Mari Sandoz's biography, a book that would haunt me, in an

American studies course during a vulnerable spring term at
Michigan State. April has always knocked me for a not very
pleasant loop where my brain seems semifevered. Here I was
in crowded East Lansing terminally homesick and missing
the trout fishing opener April twenty-third and thus the
woeful history of Crazy Horse and the Sioux was a gut
punch. Now here I am forty years later and my mind again
becomes that of a twenty-year-old college junior writing a
term paper speculating that both Crazy Horse and the
Apache leader Geronimo were motivated toward war by the
deaths of their three-year-old children who died because we
simply enough were chasing their people to death. It is said
that Crazy Horse spent three days with his deceased daughter on her burial platform in a tree playing with her toys.

   I left the windows open in the gathering heat and
walked the scant thirty yards to the death site but then my
eyes blurred with tears and I returned to the car. Marybelle
was stretching feline style.

   "I'm not going to ask you where we are. I need some
new light on the nature of reality. I also need some coffee.
This fucking sunburn itches. I also need to pee."

   "I wouldn't get optimistic on reality." I poured her
coffee from the thermos.

   A little while later when a sign gave us a hearty welcome to Wyoming I stopped the car and we got out to study
this border. Obviously it lacked the specificity of the jigsaw
puzzle where Nebraska was green and then there was suddenly the blue of Wyoming which to the eye lacked blue
except the sky. The earth herself lacked any sign of demar-
cation. There was an urge to walk to a distant butte, sit

down, and think things over but then I judged the butte to be a half dozen miles away. The new laser instruments surveyors use could give a reading on the border that was accurate to a thousandth of an inch. It didn't used to be such a science and when the new technology came in I lost forty feet of woods on the north end of the farm but picked up twenty feet of good pasture to the east though when I talked to my neighbors none of us was up to building new fences.

"I've failed as a wife and a mother," Marybelle said when I got back to the car. I didn't know the details so I couldn't respond. She sniffed and then picked up the road atlas for the first time on the trip. "We have to detour up to Malta before you drop me in Bozeman. I need to make some apologies."

I slowed to a near stop and located Malta up toward the northern border of Montana. It was fine by me and I turned to her but she was snoozing again. When I had applied the vinegar she said she had taken a sleeping pill or two. Vivian used to drink this over-the-counter sleeping potion and still say she didn't sleep a wink but then I knew otherwise because she was so dead to the world she didn't even get up to pee. My doctor, AD, says women need more sleep these days as their lives are often fraught with tension of an undetermined source. On a day when I was hauling bull calves to the sale yard Vivian was all wound up in a frazzle trying to sell a cottage for twice what it was worth a few years back. People who come from downstate have so much money they buy their kids brand-new cars.

Marybelle is obsessed with her fatigue. It's different for me because I know the future is more of the same. However, this may have changed now what with my past life being cut off by the sale of the farm. When I wake up at first light I still wake up as a farmer. I think of doing morning chores that are no longer there for me. Lola would help me break up bales of hay with her teeth. The cattle would stand around her as if in full approval. Twenty-five years of routine and suddenly it's evening.

What can my dad give me now? Maybe that I should loosen up as much as I am able. And stop thinking of that little farm on the Niobrara about ten miles from Valentine. Everyone pretty much pans out in the middle ground or less. In college I thought I was destined to go overseas but I didn't. We don't quite get started except on our livelihood which is probably the story of mankind. This doesn't include what realtors like Vivian call "lucky sperms," those with a bunch of inherited wealth. In some of the rest of us hope keeps springing up like rye grass. Marybelle says that if her husband can wangle a teaching job in a big urban area she can "return to the life of the little theater." Instead of model airplanes my son Robert used to make cardboard models of theaters, sort of theater dollhouses. He even made a little mock-up of Shakespeare's old-timey theater in London, the Globe, and won a 4-H blue ribbon for it at the county fair.

Thinking was wearing me out so I stopped the car to take a photo of some grand-looking Angus bulls up on a hillside near a rock outcropping. When I walked up the hill they weren't too happy with my presence and the largest began to paw and blow snot so I retreated. I owned a tough old bull I named Bob and Lola liked to tease him until he'd bellow in fury, but then later she might take a nap in the shade of his huge body and several times on especially hot days I watched from the kitchen window as they strolled out to the pond together for a dip. I've always had this notion that we don't know other mammals nearly as well as we pretend to.

Back in the car I got a boner glancing at Marybelle's butt peeking out of the bottom of the T-shirt and speculated if I put on three condoms it would likely protect my slowly healing member. The contrast here and there of white and sunburned skin was hunky-dory erotic. I felt like a geezer Peeping Tom and turned back to the road atlas with prickly heat in my wattles, refusing to admit that good luck is a mixed blessing. My friend AD had insisted that I see the Wind River and the Sunlight Basin but that was way over west and out of the way to a more direct route to Malta. Wisdom told me to drive to Malta in Montana, head south to Bozeman, and rid myself of this nutcase woman who was blinding me to the beauty of the United States, but even as I thought this my weary eyes would flicker from map to bottom to map to bottom. A couple of times a year when Robert was in Arizona he'd send me a five-pound bag of prime pistachios. He thought that the tyranny pistachios had over me was funny. There was an obvious connection over pistachios which I'd eat until nearly in tears and Marybelle's stellar bottom.

Suddenly it occurred to me that I hadn't rid myself of the Nebraska piece of the puzzle and here I was fifty miles into Wyoming. I pulled off on the bumpy shoulder of the road waking Marybelle who hissed "fuck head" meaning me I suppose. Across the ditch there was a small irrigation

channel and I released Nebraska with its tiny picture of
an ear of corn to float merrily down the man-made stream.
I squinted my eyes making the ditch look like a giant river
and I was a hawk flying above it, or more likely a flycatcher
like a black phoebe, and then Marybelle's feet were beside
me and she sat down in the ditch.

"Wow, this feels great on my sunburn," she said. I
glanced up and a rancher passed in an ancient gray
Studebaker pickup and we waved at each other. Marybelle
lay back in the ditch and rolled over and over like a porpoise might. The water felt pretty cold to me but who was I
to say so? A little while later we had breakfast in Shawnee
at a place where the Studebaker was parked and the
rancher, a small wiry man about my age, said, "There's no
charge for your girlfriend taking her morning bath in my
ditch." I thanked him and we began to talk about hay prices.
I couldn't get more than thirty bucks a ton for my alfalfa so
that's why I bought cattle. He said hay was more than twice
that locally and if you didn't raise your own you couldn't
afford to raise cows. Marybelle ate six fried eggs and three
sausage patties. The waitress, a big older woman, was
amazed and Marybelle nodded at me and said, "This old fool
keeps me up all night and I'm hungry." I was a little embarrassed when the waitress and rancher laughed loudly.

MONTANA

I made tracks for Montana, hitting Interstate 25 over past Douglas and heading north toward Casper and Billings. Marybelle had become a herky-jerky chatterbox holding her cell phone at the ready for a signal. I questioned her sudden energy and she said she was getting a protein rush from her eggs and sausage. I said that was only a half hour ago and it wasn't possible unless she was a dog because they can metabolize fat and protein real fast.

"Cliff, I know my body real well, thank you, and I'm getting a protein rush."

I let it go because I recalled how marital arguments can start with tiny seeds and grow instantaneously into giant oaks. I had also accepted as fact that I wouldn't see the "real America" with my present passenger. For instance I had neglected to say that Wyoming, receding into the past, is known as the equality state, the western meadowlark her bird, the motto "Equal Rights," and the wildflower the Indian paintbrush, a flower I have loved since childhood.

Near Douglas Marybelle as a joke called my cell phone but it was turned off and in my suitcase in the back so the joke went flat. She was irked and gave me a lecture on cell phone ethics.

"Cliff, a cell phone isn't a toy. It's a very lucky technical miracle for all of us. It's a prime weapon against our essential loneliness."

"I can't say I ever felt that lonely." I knew it was a mistake to say this but I couldn't help myself.

"Bullshit. You're utterly lonely without knowing it. You wandered around that farm in a state of absolute loneliness. I bet you talked more to your dog than to your wife."

"Vivian got so she mostly wanted to talk about real estate and maybe a little about whatever diet she was on."

"The question is, did you try to get interested in her issues? Maybe real estate is more creative than farming?"

"That's certainly possible." I was trying to look for a route to back away.

"Right now you're high and dry and I sense you're vaguely looking for a creative solution to your life but are you really searching?"

"I have a few things in mind that haven't quite taken shape." I was miffed, glancing back between the front seats to see that Marybelle had put her suitcase smack dab on top of the puzzle.

"Name one!" she fairly hissed. "Name one single creative thought you've had for your future!"

"Well, when you slept all that time I did some thinking. I've mostly been working since I was twelve years old.
My mother was made of iron and used to say, 'Idle hands
are the devil's work tools.' On the other hand my dad was
real playful. Sometimes you wonder how they got together
in the first place. Anyway, once when I was fishing the
Jordan River with my dad we watched a family of otter at
play and he explained that otters were so intelligent and
skilled that they didn't have to work hard to get their food.
They spent a great deal of time fooling around, sliding down
steep banks like kids on sleighs and teasing other less for-
tunate creatures."

"Step on the gas. I don't see where you're going with
this idea."

I could see she was getting antsy because we were
coming close to Casper and she had a top-flight signal on
her phone.

"When you were bathing like a porpoise in that irrigation ditch I was also watching a pair of ravens. Like otters
they have the privilege of fooling around a lot. So do por-
poises or so I've read. So do people if they don't just work
forty-eight years like I did. So I had this idea at breakfast
that I would start this project of renaming the birds of North
America, and also the names of the states. Some of both are
okay but most fall short of having the right names."

"I don't fucking believe it, you goof."

Marybelle acted poleaxed but not to the degree she
couldn't dial her friend in Minneapolis. I drove off an exit
on the freeway to take a look at the Platte River not wanting to listen to the conversation. When I got out of the car

she covered the mouthpiece and said, "It's an intriguing idea but I doubt if it's marketable."

The river was moving from left to right. I had thought about tying my little ninety-pound dinghy rowboat to the top of the car but it was cumbersome except for short trips to local ponds and little lakes. Lola would sit on the backseat as if we were doing something of tremendous importance. Maybe she was right. I moved further away from the car so as not to hear any ambient chatter. Rivers make my favorite sound. If I had brought along my rowboat I could have escaped confusion because when you row you tend to think about nothing except the world floating off behind you. Staring at the river I began to wonder what we are when we are alone. Maybe we don't count for much unless we are rubbing against others. I recalled that way back when in college when I was reading Thoreau I discovered he didn't spend all that much time at that shack he built near Walden Pond. My dad had to interfere when I was too much alone in the spring of my sophomore year in high school. I was sweet on the prettiest girl in the whole school. She was a newcomer, a preacher's daughter who arrived with her parents in the middle of winter. Her dad was a Nazarene fundamentalist and was too big a rock to last for long on the little shelf of our community. Every boy in high school was after Rebecca and it was inevitable that she would land in the lap of our best athlete who was a brutal lout with a big dick, common knowledge because the showers in our locker room were wide open. Anyway, I was close to Rebecca only once and that was when we drew lots to see who would partner on Spring Cleaning

Day when we walked along the roads with big garbage
bags picking up the trash thrown out of cars, mostly beer
cans and bottles. I was thought to be the luckiest boy in
school for drawing Rebecca who all the boys referred to
as P.T. (prick tease) though never to her face. This was a
period of miniskirts though Rebecca was never allowed by
her parents to wear one. She made up for this by throwing herself around in longer skirts giving us all a peek of
what was widely called "the promised land" with a lack of
modesty similar to Marybelle's in present time. When
Rebecca and I were dropped off on a small gravel road
through a swamp it was disappointing that she was wearing loose trousers for the duty work of picking up trash. I
was burning up with lust, love, and embarrassment but
she was remote and lazy letting me do all the work because
she was afraid of the spiders but mostly garter snakes. I
found a stick in the grass on the road's shoulder for her to
carry and she sang religious songs ("Just as I am without
one plea . . .") for further protection against nature. At one
point she called me over and poked at a used condom des-
iccating on the gravel on the road's edge. She rolled her
eyes and giggled while my heart rose thumping in my
throat. The high point for my hormonal fantasies occurred
when we were nearly finished. She began shrieking and
dancing around saying that there were spiders crawling up
her legs. She yelled, "Don't look" and pulled her trousers
down to her knees and started slapping at her legs, glanced
at me and hissed, "Get away asshole," which was startling
for a religious girl. I was frozen in place and stared as in-
tensely as possible at her pubic mound and furze peeking

out beneath white cotton panties. She swiveled and asked, "Is there one on my butt?" I dropped to my knees, my eyes only inches from her tulip fanny. "A very small one," I whispered, watching a tiny spider traverse the upper back of her thigh. "Kill it," she screeched and I did so with a trembling fingertip. And then it was over, this high point of my erotic life thus far.

It's strange how memories can arrive in swarms like bees. Memories are obviously one thing we have all to ourselves. Rebecca lost her cherry and got knocked up by the lout athlete through the well-known trick of vodka and orange juice. I was so bereft I couldn't bear human company. I ignored my studies for final exams that May and walked in the woods with our mongrel terrier Fred. By mid-June Dad took me aside to explain the "facts of life." He was irked because I didn't even want to go fishing on Sunday morning. He said, "Don't go after the prettiest girl. It's like pissing in the wind. Besides, they make the decision and if it's not you there's nothing to do about it. By and large the prettiest girl in town is a curse on the life of the male she picks."

Suddenly Marybelle was behind me and I was looking at her with the eyes of a fifteen-year-old sophomore. Dad was wrong in that you can't aim your desire like a rifle during deer season. Desire isn't subject to logic. For instance Marybelle looked attractive in her short pale blue skirt until she said that her friend in Minneapolis was having "sexual issues" at which point she became a zombie and lunch was a better idea than the grandest fuck in the history of mankind. Ever present was the cultural fantasy that you could separate the fuck from the fuckers.

I ate alone at the tavern on the outskirts of Casper. I
promised to bring a sandwich to Marybelle who had had a
sudden insight on her friend's problems and was back on
her pink phone with her bare toes doing pit-a-pat on the
windshield. I had one of the top five burgers in my life (un-
frozen half-pound patty) and listened to cowboys, ranchers, and townspeople, many of whom were drinking their
late lunch, talk about the current political situation. In the
past couple of years I had learned to favor the raving opin-
ions of drinkers over newspaper and television pundits. The
drinkers could be nonsensical ("Halliburton is giving
George Bush one billion dollars the day he finishes his second term") but had the virtue of being fresher and more
original than the pundits who always inferred they had
sources unavailable to the rest of us even though their secret sources apparently had nothing new to say. The excep-
tion seemed to be the columns of Frank Rich and the late
Molly Ivins that my son Robert faxed me through Vivian's
real estate office. My government reminded me of nothing
so much as the fraternities way back when at Michigan
State. The 95 percent of us that didn't take part in "Greek
life" were outside the pall. There was little or no communication between our two worlds.

When I brought out Marybelle's sandwich (peanut
butter and strawberry jam) she was serenely happy. Her
friend would meet us in Bozeman and drive back to Minnesota with Marybelle.

"I think a road trip would do Marcia a world of good.
I mean our trip has been really stimulating me. I mean I was

just sitting there in Minnesota hitting the tranqs and brooding about my future and now, surprise, I'm in Casper."

   I felt too good in the aftermath of my first-rate burger
to want to deal with big issues. I nodded to a herd of Angus
out in a pasture in silent thanks that they taste so good.

MONTANA II

"These reading glasses have always made me think more deeply."

We were passing a Wyoming town with the peculiar name of Kaycee. Marybelle was sitting there in the gun seat having won our first serious argument at the end of which I had felt the deepest sympathy for her husband. Now she was posing as a stenographer with the glasses tilted down her nose as if they were bifocals. The upshot was that she insisted on helping me on my "creative project" of renaming birds and states. This pissed me off since the idea had long been a private little amusement for the boredom of tractor time, or the weeks of pruning cherry trees on cold and windy March days. I considered it as a piece of silliness I shared only with Lola who was quite interested in anything I said.

"Wordsworth wrote alone," I had said, perhaps the weakest straw I could grasp since I could remember almost nothing about Wordsworth except a visual image of him flouncing around the Lake District.

"You're wrong there, kiddo. His sister Dorothy was right there beside him for every line he wrote."

"Oh bullshit," I had said even though college was closer in time for Marybelle and she perhaps remembered things about Wordsworth that had slipped my mind. She then headed for the peripheries as Vivian always did during a quarrel. I had thought of this tactic as Indians circling a wagon train before dashing in to scalp the woeful pioneers who were already suffering from cholera. For instance, if Vivian wanted to go to a Saturday night polka party and she sensed that I didn't she might begin by criticizing that I always wore the same thing to polka parties (a lightweight green Hawaiian shirt Robert had sent me from Maui). As Vivian grew larger she used a smaller voice, nearly the kind of baby talk used on puppies and human babies. It was hard on the nerves when the volume rose during quarrels.

Marybelle's attack was more sophisticated and intended to exhaust her prey before the kill. She suggested that I had given Lola the name Lola because of the scandalous novel by Nabokov called *Lolita*. I said no, the name came from that absurd song "Whatever Lola Wants, Lola Gets." Anyone who taught school knows that seventh grade girls are the nastiest critters in the school yard and are well beyond romantic or erotic interest.

She took another tack saying that I obviously needed therapy to "draw me out" from my solitary profession of farming. She herself had been in therapy for twenty years which enabled her to communicate with everyone except

possibly her own daughter and husband. Marybelle then did
an end run returning to Dorothy Wordsworth without
whom the poet would have been nothing.

"We haven't exactly been brother and sister," I
contended.

"Men always bring up sex when they're at a loss. I call
that dick thinking."

I was trapped in this whirl of the irrational. Sensing victory she took out her deep-thinking glasses and a tiny note-
book and an orange pen with a grinning clown head. My
limited imagination went dead on birds and states. I remembered a morning in March when the northern world was icy
slush and I had a stupid conversation with Babe, my waitress lover. We began arguing about snow depths and like most
people she remembered a fictional past when the great north
was suffocated in snow every winter. I used a line I remembered from my college Shakespeare class and paraphrased
clumsily, "You have but a woman's reason, you think it so because you think it so." The diner fell silent and people stopped
eating their health-giving biscuits with sausage gravy. I sensed
that my smart mouth had gotten me into deep shit. To get out
of this jam I had to buy Babe an iPod so she could listen to
country music on her morning walks. Without this gift there
would be no sex, an act she called "making the two-backed
beast," also from Shakespeare without her knowing it.

All of these dark thoughts had affected the splendid
landscape between Casper and Buffalo which I dully re-
corded as if my glum mood had repainted the green hills and
snowcapped Big Horn Mountains. We drank too much
before dinner, had bad steaks and limp lettuce, and in

desperation tried to make love. When I stood in the toilet
applying the steroid ointment and slipping on three condoms
it stole my spontaneity. My weenie lost its pride and shrunk.
I left the motel room and bought a pack of Lucky Strikes, a
habit I had quit a decade before. I had two more bourbons
in a bar and reflected on the brittle silliness of life.

Dawn came bright and clear and cold, the first break in
a week of heat. Marybelle missed the Montana border in what
was doubtless a sleeping pill trance, curled up in my lined
denim coat. Montana was the treasure state, with the western meadowlark the bird (same as Wyoming), "Oro y Plata"
("Gold and Silver") the motto, and the bitterroot the flower.

I now regretted that I hadn't given Marybelle a single
imaginary bird or state name. I had stonewalled when I
should have made a joke out of it. I had ruminated like an
old cow. Now she looked like a bleak Dickens tyke, an author my students disliked because he was so "pessimistic."
My dreams had put me in a pleasant turmoil. Homeland
security had prevented me from crossing the Mississippi on
my eventual trip home back to sanity. I couldn't count to
ten or spell my name and had the dream perception that life
herself was a huge sow rooting in a swamp near the deer
camp in the U.P. What could this possibly mean except that
the sow came first and meaning later? When I was in first
grade I held a little girl piglet I named Patty and a few years
later she weighed over four hundred and drowned when she
fell through the pond ice the day before Christmas.

Because the morning was clear and cold with a stiff
breeze from the north I had the nice illusion that my thinking was clear and cold. Here I was at sixty with no home to

return to but that didn't make me unique. Time tricks us
into thinking we're part of her and then leaves us behind.
My home depended on the continuity of my marriage to
Vivian which I always assumed would only end at my death.
I also assumed I still loved her but then love can be a routine like farming. I wasn't jealous when she expressed sexual
desire for an actor in a TV movie so maybe my love had
faded? My friend AD had said that toward the end of a
marriage you're like a rat trapped in a septic tank.

When I pulled into the parking lot of the Little Bighorn
Battlefield National Monument at Crow Agency, Montana,
I lightly shook Marybelle who had casually exposed a pretty
good knowledge of American history. She looked at the Park
Service signs with sleepy disgust. "Custer was a murderous
peacock who mistreated his men, wife, and dogs," she said
and promptly went back to sleep.

I was a solitary wanderer on the battlefield and was
quite amazed at the markers that signified exactly where
each of our brave or perhaps stupid soldiers had fallen, not
that it mattered if the authorities were off a few feet. Not
having been in the armed services myself I had always been
a little embarrassed by such notions as "obeying orders,"
"semper fidelis," "death before dishonor," or "live free or
die." The most frequent words in the media which I tended
to avoid of late were "car bomb." I was far too distracted by
Marybelle to wonder if our current president was yet another of the many Custers who willy-nilly have littered our
history. This was the briefest of thoughts compared to the
growing fiction that Marybelle was at least three people
rather than one. Maybe we are all several people but I

doubted it. I had certainly hoped my trip would ease my
feeling of puzzlement but it hadn't so far.

All of the graves on the green hillside drew me back to
the idea that at my age of sixty you could drop dead at any
moment. Weather-wise was it autumn or early winter in my
life? My jacket was too short and I could feel the cold wind
in my kidneys. Just before I left AD had cooked dinner for
me but he had confessed to drinking two bottles of expensive wine and the stew was glutinous. I somewhat dreaded
AD's after-dinner conversations because he could have a
glass of French apple brandy and sit back in his La-Z-Boy
chair and assume the posture of a wise old owl. He would
say some sensible things but then drop a sentence similar
to opening your freezer and finding a chopped-up muskrat.
He had said, in effect, "Yours is an American story. You lose
your life's long-term substance, your wife and farm and dog.
You are cut loose. At your age you can't think of new worlds
to conquer or big-deal adventures in far-flung places. The
only real adventure in most people's life is adultery."

There you have it. On the bare grassy battlefield I
thought of my pleasant feelings about Wordsworth's *The
Prelude* as a college junior but couldn't pin down any par-
ticulars. It was like playing horseshoes. You had to keep
at it. About a hundred yards away I could see the top of
Marybelle's head through the car's front window and wasn't
sure if I wanted to return to the car which put me back in
the dubious battlefield of answered prayers. You tie biology to the imagination and you can have a mud bath. Forty-
five years of sex fantasies come true and I'm thinking that I
wish I could go fishing.

MONTANA III

I laughed when I got back in the car. After more than a week of sweltering here I was shivering as if I had just left my ice shanty over on Mullett Lake. Marybelle seemed cozy enough in my jacket but there were goose bumps on her pretty legs (she had a trampoline in her backyard). I had a cup of weak thermos coffee, lit a courageous Lucky Strike, had a coughing fit, and studied the road atlas. Montana was a big-assed state but with any luck I'd be done with my passenger in two days. At the top of the page the information revealed that Montana was three times the size of Michigan but with only one-tenth in population, though in truth most of Michigan's population was down in the bottom third of the mitten (the shape of the state). Of course it's hard to draw conclusions from maps or from the dozens of stories I read as a boy about Montana in outdoor magazines wherein a vast slavering grizzly bear charged a tiny hunter whose rifle looked like a Tinkertoy in his hands. In terms of artistic perspective the bear in the illustration would have weighed two tons and the man fifty pounds. Another thing that seemed to happen in Montana is alarmed fishermen in boats unwittingly plunging over waterfalls and clinging to rocks downriver. If they survived they started a fire with waterproof matches to dry out until Ranger Rick found them. In short, Montana was fraught with sporting peril though contemporary versions of the sporting magazines used words like "sustainable" and "megafauna."

Driving north toward Billings with my antique Taurus buffeted by the wind I began to think of Robert's last trip home for Christmas the year before the disaster. To humor me we had gone ice fishing first stopping at a dealer's to buy him a snowmobile suit and moon boots to keep him warm. Were it not for the aqua foulard at his throat he would have looked like a normal dumpy ice fisherman. Our traditional Christmas Eve dinner was fried panfish (bluegills and perch) when the lake ice was solid enough to fish. By midmorning it was only ten degrees but I had a fire going in the shanty and had set out a legal number of tip-ups after spudding the holes, taking turns with Robert who had always been strong as an ox and said he went to a gym four days a week.

Anyway, the sun came out by late morning and Robert put on these big polarized goggles that covered half his face and had cost him a hundred bucks. It was a little like talking to someone from outer space. Fishing was slow which left us plenty of time to chat and I said farming had become less pleasant because of erratic market pressures.

Sweet and sour cherries would never recover from the over-
planting after a couple of good years two decades before
when big money entered the business. We were outproducing
the market by 10 percent. Beef was in fine shape but mostly
because we had embargoed Canada due to mad cow disease.
Robert asked me what I had netted this year and I was
embarrassed to say nineteen grand. He said, "Dad, that's
shit," but then a tip-up flag signaled a fish and Robert was
joyful pulling up a fat foot-long perch, his favorite. When
he calmed down I was subjected to a grueling number of
business questions including the suggestion that I put the
farm "to sleep" and go back to teaching. I didn't say "What
would old Lola do all day without me?" but said I'd rather
get a brain tumor than go back to teaching. Robert was irritated that Vivian wasn't kicking in some of the real estate
money she was saving for our retirement. We let my dire
situation drop and he told amusing horror stories about the
movie business and the berserk market pressures and how
in the manner of farming they invented "crops" no one
wanted. The real bomb was dropped at noon when we were
eating our baked bean and raw onion sandwiches and he
admitted he had been averaging more than three hundred
thousand dollars a year. It was incomprehensible that my
whimsical, wayward son could make that kind of money.
He said that since he was destined to have no heirs himself
I should let him know when I needed money. On the way
home we stopped at a tavern in Boyne City where we knew
everyone and Robert announced loudly, "I too am an American sportsman," and the drinkers cheered. They all knew
his sexual predilections but then again he was "local."

When we were coming down the hill into Billings Marybelle yelled "Mom" in her sleep. This was a little alarming but I was too impressed by the Yellowstone River to be concerned. The river was too huge to be believed. The watersheds in Michigan are fairly short so I was unused to vast rivers except for crossing the Mississippi up in Minneapolis when we took the 4-H kids on a junket to the Minnesota State Fair and I hadn't paid much attention what with trying to stop neckers from coupling in the school bus.

I was so fascinated with the bigness of the Yellowstone that I missed my turnoff for Malta but a hasty look at the map revealed a second option. Meanwhile a few miles past Columbus I pulled off on the shoulder, climbed a fence and walked through a herd of Angus heifers down a hill to the river which was so loud and turbulent I couldn't hear myself think. I'm sort of neutral in terms of religion but ever since I was a kid I've thought moving water to be the best thing God made. Back in grade school when I started trout fishing with my dad he told me that gods and spirits lived in creeks and rivers, information he got from his own father's Chippewa buddy. I never doubted this one bit. Where else would they live?

I was standing there in tall grass on the riverbank when I thought I heard the buzz of a rattlesnake and I jumped sky-high. It turned out to be the cell phone Marybelle insisted that I carry in my baggy pants pocket. I took it out and tried to figure what button to press, my heart still beating wildly from the fake snake. When I said "Hello" she said "We don't have a good signal" and hung up. I waved up at her where she leaned against the car drinking coffee. I was

tempted to pitch the phone in the river but then I'd only have
to buy another one.

On the way up the hill to the car it occurred to me that
I might feel a vacuum after I dropped her off. She smiled then
astonished me by singing a song in a high pure voice but the
end was drowned out by a semi carrying a load of Kohler toilet
bowls. A few minutes later when we stopped at Reed Point
for breakfast, an early lunch, because she was "famished"
she explained that during her two years at Sarah Lawrence
before she "stupidly" eloped she was a member of a choral
group that sang ancient music. I told her that I admired her
perfect pitch and the rare ability to sing so beautifully without accompaniment. Having no talents myself I was silly with
admiration for someone who did. While Marybelle was eating her six eggs, sausage, and potatoes, I told her about a little
round girl who had been a student of mine, a ninth grader,
the first year I taught. She was from a very poor family,
"trailer trash" as mean-minded students called such students. Emma was her name and when we were studying
Emily Dickinson she shyly offered her own versions which I
thought were extraordinary. She always smelled like potatoes fried in bacon fat which I guessed was a major part of
her family's diet. By the spring of that year her family had
moved south to Flint in hopes that her dad could get work
and that was the end of Emma in my life. In June when I
passed their ramshackle mobile home on the edge of the state
forest the door was open and flapping and the ragweed,
nettles, and thistles were three feet high in the yard.

The story infuriated Marybelle who said she "deeply"
identified with Emma. I didn't quite get the connection but

said nothing. Marybelle's anger passed into laughter when we left the restaurant and on the way out through the foyer there was a poster advertising a Reed Point festival called "The Running of the Sheep," an evident takeoff on the running of the bulls in Pamplona. There were photos of senior-citizen men chasing sheep down an alley while spectators drank beer. Marybelle began to say something predictably nasty about Hemingway, dropped the idea, and trilled a passage of a song from old-time Italy. I mean it wasn't loud but soft and dulcet and served to calm my mind though my tummy and lower down were a mess and I had to skip lunch.

A man in the restaurant explained that the immense size of the river was due to the melting snow in the mountains accelerated by the recent heat wave. He directed us to a park across the river and I felt uneasy crossing the bridge, doubting its stability. I was more than pleased to see the port-a-potty. To Marybelle's credit she noted that I was feeling ill. When I had stopped for gas early in the morning the station had a self-service snack bar called a "Nuke feast" where I heated up a sausage sandwich in a radar range. The sandwich was currently attacking my gizzard and in between trips to the port-a-potty I lay out on a sleeping bag, drank a gallon of water, and at my request Marybelle kept singing the ancient songs accompanied by the turbulent music of the river in front of us. I greeted a floating cottonwood tree that passed by at top speed with a group of blackbirds sitting on the trunk for a free ride. Marybelle would glance at her cell phone in hopes for a signal but lucky for me none arose.

My thoughts, a bit deranged by my semifevered discomfort, turned oddly to ice fishing with Robert. He had said that some of the neurotic unrest felt by actors and actresses came from the idea that they didn't write their own lines. They were performing vehicles for someone else's work. When the script was good everyone tended to be happy. When the script was bad chaos reigned though the best of the acting profession could do pretty well even with a bad scenario up to a point. What bothered me on the sleeping bag listening to Marybelle and the river was the idea that with my clumsy consent my own script and most of the human race's had been written for us.

MONTANA IV

It was midafternoon before I was able to travel. As always with illness, however slight, I became a little tender-minded. In my youth the only time my mother was soft and kind and gentle to me was when I was sick. When I got measles she was a Sister of Eternal Mercy and Love. When I was well she saved it all for my little brother with Down's. Dad joked that "Iron Greta" was made in a drop forge. Last year at our local voting place at the Grange Hall a rickety old lady in her late eighties teased me that in the fifties she used to be "sweet" on my dad down in Mancelona. I laughed and told her that I hoped they had a good time. When she tottered out with her sullen nose-ringed granddaughter she giggled and said that my dad was a "randy rascal."

I couldn't let Marybelle drive because her glances at her cell phone for a signal were relentless. In our three hours or so at the river's beach in Reed Point she referred

to herself as Nurse Nancy but back in the car she became
brittle and petulant. When we stopped at a rest area so she
could pee a small lightbulb went off in my mind when it
occurred to me that she was a cross between two women I
had desired for years. I found that I uniformly liked the
women in television lotion ads, and one Jergens lady in
particular. My all time favorite was a young woman with
an Irish setter in a mattress ad which Lola also liked because
of the dog. Marybelle seemed a genetic fusion of these two
sources of lust. There was a question if television made my
lust artificial? My friend AD said that sex in a nontraditional
society was always up for grabs. It was like tennis with no
net played in a gravel pit. The wisdom of this was moder-
ated by what I had learned on the phone south of Minneapolis vis-à-vis AD asking a woman to pee in his hat. Where
did this come from?

A certain amount of shit hit the fan when I turned north
on 191 in Big Timber bound for ever-distant Malta. We
stopped on the far side of a bridge over the Yellowstone
because Marybelle was bound to lose her signal farther on.
Her first call to Minneapolis made her sob. She spoke to the
husband of her dear friend and found out that this "sister"
was in a clinic for severe depression and was presently un-
reachable. I fled the car having thought I could doze through
a long chat about "issues." I also felt squeamish knowing the
next call would be to her daughter and husband up on their
dig near Malta. Marybelle had said that this dig was far from
her husband's interest in possible Native American cannibalism but he was helping out a friend from the University
of Nebraska who was always struggling for tenure.

The day had turned warmish and there was a profuse bug hatch above the brown and roiling Yellowstone. There must have been a hundred swallows swooping around and feeding on the insects. It's impossible to watch a swallow fly and not want to be one at least for a while. To the southwest of me were the snowcapped Absaroka Mountains and to the northwest the Crazy Mountains whose peaks were creamy with snow. I had the idea that on this trip I'd climb the first mountain of my life though I'd have to inquire about proper footwear and suchlike.

My sweat was coolish and I felt giddy lighting a cigarette, a habit I was able to quit when I quit teaching. Back then the teachers who smoked went down to the furnace room for a few quick puffs between classes. Though some now consider smoking the equivalent of baby raping it can be a contemplative activity. I was suddenly quite lonely for my workshop, a shed attached to the barn and calving shed. It was hard to leave my tools behind for the auction. I only saved my dad's favorite hammer. So much of it was sentimental junk: half of a once favorite pliers, a broken fence stretcher, a nail puller, the head of an adze, a full can of paint with a label missing, a Mason jar of keys, used spark plugs in a wooden cheese box from Wisconsin that once held three-year-old cheddar, a tin can full of lantern wicks, a keg of bent nails I had meant to straighten and reuse. Once I had found a Prince Albert tobacco can full of dirty photos that Vivian's father had hidden in the back of the drawer. Old-fashioned erotic photos featuring real fleshy women in black stockings. I can't say that they were a jolt to my noodle.

I had upset the swallows but now fifteen minutes later they decided I was harmless as they brought back bugs to regurgitate for their children. I had begun to wonder if age sixty was too late to change my life not that I had any choice. The other time of radical life change was when I quit teaching in my midthirties. I thought I was pretty resilient at the time but I wasn't. I was only one of many of my generation of hippies and future yuppies who had a theory and acted it out. I was heartsick with books and teaching and wanted to simply live the "natural" life of a farmer. I let my mind life go dead. I was amused at the influx of city people in the seventies and eighties who also wanted to live a natural life in the country and who didn't realize that farming was as technical in its own way as electrical engineering. They listened to Neil Young whom I liked myself but then I knew how to farm. Last month I even threw away all but two of ten rather tattered pairs of bib overalls, and three pairs of lined Carhartt pants.

My cell phone buzzed unpleasantly and I stared at it a few moments as if I were holding a dog turd before I answered.

"Where are you when I need you?" she cried out so loudly the squawk box couldn't handle it closely.

"I'm a troll under a bridge, you know like the Three Billy Goats Gruff."

"What are you talking about you old dipshit," she fairly shrieked.

"I'm under the bridge studying swallows."

"My friend is suicidal in Minneapolis and my son is unconscious from malaria in Namibia. Help me."

And so on. As a teacher I was never much of a counse-
lor as I thought everyone was basically drowned in their
problems and doomed never to rise to the surface. A couple
of decades later I was no better. Luckily Route 191 from
Big Timber to Malta, a matter of two hundred and fifty miles
or so, was the grandest road I have ever been on. It was
comforting to leave the Alpine Crazies and Absarokas behind as they had a Swiss feeling that made you imagine Heidi
or *The Sound of Music*. I preferred the rolling cattle country
where any cows would be happy to live out their short lives
with higher mountain peaks in the remote distance. The
Herefords I had owned years ago were too lazy to climb a
hill for good grass and I judged that that was one reason the
breed wasn't popular out here.

A couple hours later we were passing through Judith
Gap when Marybelle decided she could improve her mood
if we made love. On leaving Big Timber she had dropped
the same kind of tranquilizer, Zoloft, that Vivian had used
in dire straits. I wasn't too enthused but drove off the highway onto a small gravel ranch road until we reached higher
hills and I parked near a meadow and aspen thicket. We
walked through a cattle gate with Marybelle shedding her
summer shift and standing there in panties and sneakers.
Suddenly she took off running up the hill and into the aspen
thicket and I remembered she had been quite the track star
in high school. There was no chance of me catching her so
I got my camera out of the car and took photos of three
Charolais bulls glowering at me from across the fence line.
After about fifteen minutes an older woman came by on horse-
back with two Australian shepherds that weren't friendly.

She told me I was trespassing and pointed at red paint on
the post and I apologized saying that we used signs in Michigan. I added that the bit of red paint was pleasanter to the
eye than "No Trespassing" signs. I then explained that my
girlfriend had run off up the hill and would she mind taking a look. We could see Marybelle about a mile up the steep
hill beyond the aspens in a swatch of meadow. The woman
and her dogs took off at an alarming speed. They were back
in ten minutes with Marybelle seminude and grinning behind the woman who was angry and said, "Shame on you
for being mean to her, you shithead geezer." I couldn't think
of a thing to say in my defense.

We reached Malta in the last light after driving one
hundred and thirty stupendous miles from Lewistown.
When we crossed the Missouri I sang "Across the Wide
Missouri" which amused Marybelle who had been in a good
mood since her uphill run. However, the only line I knew
was the title line. I also took a photo of a golden eagle on a
fence post not thirty feet away.

I was still a little queasy from my rotten dawn sausage
and this was added to by the idea of meeting Marybelle's
husband and daughter, Brad and Sara, as we neared Malta.
What would I say? Pleased to meet you. We found the shabby
little motel with muddy old SUVs parked in front. A group
of men and one girl were sitting around a small campfire on
the grass.

"Mom!" the girl yelled and came running to the car
followed by a short man in khakis. The three of them embraced and I stood there as if fascinated by the mosquito

near my nose. We were introduced and dad and daughter were direct and friendly which still didn't calm my quavery mind and tummy. The husband, Brad, and Marybelle walked off down an alley and I told the daughter I needed a drink. She pointed out a bar across the street.

"You were mom's all-time favorite teacher," she said.

"I hope your brother in Africa is feeling better," I said lamely for want of anything better. We were at the saloon door and I was desperate for a double.

"There is no brother." She paused before opening the door. "She and Dad split up for a year when I was three. I stayed in Kansas with Dad and she went off to New York. She told Dad she had an abortion and ever since then I've been blessed with an imaginary brother."

I drank a double whiskey while digesting this, imagining there might also be something wrong with Bozeman. There was. The cousin giving her a car in Bozeman was fictional.

"Mom goes on these affection binges about once a year. Dad puts up with it. He's from a Quaker family and wouldn't think of divorce. Compared to other academic couples they're not that unhappy."

She sensed that I was completely knocked off my balance and put her hand in mine. I had a mediocre cheeseburger (frozen patty) and we played a few games of pool. She was a little shorter than Marybelle and very handsome. She said she had a few boyfriends but was headed for MIT in the fall where she had been awarded a graduate fellowship. "I love rocks," she said. "Naturally I worry about Mom and Dad but they've been doing this dance for twenty-two years." She pointedly questioned me and when I said I had forty-five more states to cover she said "Cool."

I was mildly tipsy when she led me back across the street to the motel. They had rented a small room with a linoleum floor for me. It reminded me of my childhood. I loved it.

IDAHO

I awoke at 3:00 a.m. with the unpleasant smell of bourbon and onions in the room from my breath. I had an irritating hard-on when what I wished to be was a monk in a cool room reading a Latin text by candlelight. I struggled to reshape my mind to get rid of the image of Marybelle's son in darkest Africa in a malarial coma, or her rich, unpleasant cousin wondering if she really should give Marybelle her old car. How do we truly get rid of untruths? When I stopped for gas in Lewistown yesterday late afternoon I saw an item in the Great Falls newspaper saying that 85 percent of our troops in Iraq believe that Saddam was behind 9/11 even though this is demonstrably untrue.

While drinking three glasses of cold water which made my chest and head ache I had a craving for books that I hadn't had in the thirty years back when I still believed that books might save my life. That was before I quit teaching and had

decided that if I read one more book such as Norman Mailer's
Advertisements for Myself, my head would blow apart like John
Kennedy's. I went back to bed after looking out the window
to the south where I hoped to see the constellation Delta Corvi
but it was hidden by tall lilac bushes. Instead, in my mind's
eye I saw Marybelle running up the hill in her undies which
gave a twitch to my meaningless hard-on. I only began to smile
when I remembered that I was liberated from her.

It was almost but not quite that easy. I slid out of the
room shortly after 5:00 a.m. when the first birds began to
tweet. Lights were on in three other rooms and when I
reached my car door Marybelle appeared from the shadows
with a Styrofoam cup of strong coffee. I smelled the coffee
before I saw her.

"These fucking androids get up early," she giggled. "I
was hoping you'd stick around for a day and see the dig. You
know you're old and Brad doesn't see you as a threat."

"I slowly figured out that you were the pansexual one
not him," I joked.

"You might say that. I'll miss your dick more than your
lame advice. And remember to keep your cell phone charged
and on. That one attachment is so you can charge it in your
cigarette lighter in the car. I know I'll need to talk to you."

It was getting lighter fast. Sara came out in her nightie
and handed me another cup of coffee and a tortilla and beans
in a napkin. I kissed Marybelle's chastely proffered hand.
Sara rolled her eyes. I noted that the tips of her titties under
her nightie were a bit sharper than her mom's and then I
drove off with the unprofound thought of the hopelessness

of sex to improve the human condition. Perhaps I should drive to New York City and announce this to the United Nations.

Driving west on Route 2 with the sun rising at my back I could hear the voice of my mom saying in an angry metallic voice, "Act your age!" A quick dawn glance in the mirror revealed a face that reminded me of what I looked like after ten days of booze and poker at deer camp. There was a strain around my eyes as if I had been hanging out at funerals. AD liked to talk about how many older men drop dead in the adulterous saddle. With typical rudeness he had told me that Vivian had left me for partly biological reasons as Fred appeared to be a better provider for the coming winter of her life. Vivian wasn't the type that kept a root cellar full of rutabagas, potatoes, and carrots like my mom who also canned too many tomatoes and dried too many apples. Vivian believed in money in the bank, my weak point. AD was always close to bankruptcy but said that he attracted women under the illusion that all doctors are rich. You can't fight biology, he insisted, and I mentally agreed having just lost out to my pecker in a big way.

I was a little distressed by my newfound solitude and searched out an NPR station, then quickly turned it off when I heard the phrase "car bomb." I looked over at the corner of the seat, now Marybelle's empty nest, and felt a sweet relief mixed with the sweat caused by the chilies in Sara's tortilla and beans. Sara had looked wonderful leaning over the pool table with her butt arched up like a cat's. Stop, I said to myself. Sara had spent half her junior year in

Mexico and said she intended to return there after graduate school. When I asked "Why?" she said you couldn't
extrapolate Mexico over a pool game in Malta, Montana,
and that I should drive down there when I was in Arizona.
She thought my project with the jigsaw puzzle "insane" but
"appealing," as good a guide as any for a life.

My recriminations over my behavior with Marybelle
weren't quite strong enough to maintain. When some ethical node in my brain would say, "Shame on you" in my
mom's voice I would also hear my dad talking about his
boyhood dog he referred to as Ralph the Brave. When his
own father had shot a midsized bear caught in the act of
eating a piglet Ralph dove into action and lost an ear which
made him always look out of balance. Ralph would retrieve
duck and grouse and keep raccoons out of the garden, find
wounded deer, and by the time he died at fourteen most of
the dogs in the township looked like him. Ralph was pretty
big but was too cagey to act big. He thought things over
before he made his moves. I was never sure if dad was honest when he said Ralph climbed apple trees because he liked
the best apples. He wouldn't eat windfalls. Ralph had also
caught a big spawning brown trout and saved my father
from starvation when they were lost overnight in the woods.
I was not one to doubt my father but I questioned how you
could starve in one night. He said, "I don't go by what's
supposed to be true but how I feel and I felt so hungry I
could have eaten the ass out of a sow. I cooked that big fish
and split it with Ralph who was proud to provide dinner.
He fathered a litter by a little stray female that hid in a hole
under the granary. One morning Ralph brought in a fawn

he had killed and you should have seen the pups tear into it. Their cute little faces were red with blood."

When I stopped for lunch in Browning on the Blackfeet Indian Reservation I recalled how much more jauntier and happier railroad workers seemed than farmers. On the way into town I had seen an Indian boy chasing a girl on a fat pony. The boy was a fast runner but he couldn't keep up. I ate a delicious round piece of fry bread with beans for lunch. My eyes began to tear up and I couldn't quite place a reason for it. I'd like to cook a pot of beans but now I didn't have a kitchen, or a dog or a wife or a farm for that matter. I suddenly felt like I had as a boy on my first descending elevator down in Grand Rapids. Who and where was the driver?

I was trying to corner my last few beans on the plate when my cell phone buzzed in my pocket.

"I need you," she said.

"I'm a long walk to the west." My tears had given me a frog in the throat.

"That's not funny, Cliff. You can't just abandon me in Malta."

I turned the phone off so that its tiny screen went to sleep. I looked up at the round, brown waitress who was quizzical about my tears.

"My dog died," I said.

"When my dog got shot for killing chickens I was about floored." She gave me my check and patted my head. I was clearly just another American fool on the loose. I turned the cell phone back on. Marybelle might have invisible snakes in her hair but she was my only human contact in the great Northwest. The phone rang immediately.

"Never, never, never turn your phone off."

"I must have pressed the wrong button."

"You lying sack of shit. I need you. You get me off. Maybe it's because I have unresolved issues with my dad and he's not that much older than you."

"Marybelle, is there nothing you won't say?" My face was full of the blood of embarrassment.

"You never tried to cornhole me. Everyone else tries it and they get their faces slapped. You're all in all pretty nice. A bit slow, but nice."

"Thanks."

"Later."

She hung up and I drove on west though in direct contrast to the improbable beauty of the south end of Glacier National Park I entered a "woe is me" attitude. That's what Dad would say if he stubbed his toe, tangled his line while fly-fishing, or came up short on beer money and Mom wouldn't give him any. "Woe is me." He wasn't much of a reader but his favorite character in all fiction was Eeyore in A. A. Milne. Once when I was a child and we were in the saloon for hamburgers after fishing Dad had a pretty woman on each knee and said, "All I ever get is thistles."

Now I wondered how he managed to think so many awful things were actually funny like the death of my brother in the ironical sea. Naturally he wept but insisted that those who love water should have the privilege of death in water. Myself, I was high and dry. Farmers always have a future which is their farm work. In winter you've got to pitch hay to your cattle. You have to shake your cherry trees, you can't let the fruit just rot. I saw the present vacuum of my future with more dread than living in a wind tunnel with Marybelle.

I was still on Route 2 when I entered the stretched chicken neck of northern Idaho. I dropped the Montana puzzle piece in the Kootenai River. Idaho herself (states are female) was red, it's known as the gem state, it's motto is "Esta Perpetua," her flower is the syringa and the bird is the mountain bluebird which I saw in a bush not ten feet away when I stopped to fish. I thought if I caught a fish I would enter a higher plane of existence. Fishing has always given me a dose of serenity and appears to work for me far better than the Valium and Zoloft Vivian takes for nonspecific torments.

I tied on a fly known as the wooly bugger and caught an undersized rainbow. I anyway no longer owned a frying pan having sent my beloved old Wagner skillet to Robert who wanted it badly. I forgot my waders and couldn't reach a riffle corner where I knew the bigger fish would be. A year ago one day I fished for fourteen hours to get over a quarrel Vivian and the visiting Robert were having over the book *The Da Vinci Code*. Robert loathed the book for aesthetic reasons and Vivian loved it because it showed Jesus was up to no good with Mary Magdalene just like other guys. Vivian was one of those women who think that men never stop silently howling for a piece of her tail. She even called Robert "a bitch." I fled the house at dawn and went trout fishing.

I headed south near Bonners Ferry for Spokane, Washington. Idaho had started poorly and I didn't have the wit or energy to improve it. A music announcer on NPR was introducing a French song and translated an expression,

"All the mornings in the world leave without returning."
This gave me the sniffles, and I said to myself, "Cliff, you
have to take a firm hold of yourself. Take a ten-mile hike,
something sensible. All your life now is new like a warm
rain after a movie."

WASHINGTON,
NOT D.C.

In my love trance I have dropped the ball on renaming many of the states and birds. I'm diverted again by memories of teaching and how one student, the dim-witted son of a vicious social worker, was especially belligerent about there being a state of Washington and also Washington D.C. The father was uniquely a right-wing social worker bent on denying the most impoverished applicants more than pennies for their diet of fried potatoes. In college when I looked at a book of van Gogh reproductions his drawing *The Potato Eaters*, reminded me of our poorer neighborhoods when I was growing up. Their kids would go to school without socks in winter and ate bread and catsup sandwiches for lunch.

When I stopped for gas in Spokane I called my son Robert in San Francisco. I also noted that I had a message from Marybelle.

"Robert, you might want to know that Washington is known as the evergreen state, and its state bird is the willow goldfinch, its flower the coast rhododendron, and the motto is 'Alki' which means 'By and By.' I don't get this part."

"Dad, it's eight in the MORNING."

"You always were a pro sleeper, son."

"You could try it. You're not FEEDING stock at dawn anymore."

"I really miss the cattle but not as much as Lola."

"Dad, whatever you WERE you aren't anymore. I thought your road trip might help tell you that."

"I was thrown off balance by this young woman. I mean she's forty-three but that's maybe too young for me."

"Dad, even in my world you can't SKIP two generations. I mean I've never been a chicken hawk."

"Pardon?"

"Never mind. Anyway, your Marybelle called me. She made a good case that you NEED professional help. When you get here to San Francisco you're going to sit still and talk to an analyst friend of mine every single day."

"How did she get your number?"

"Off your cell phone or you wrote it down and she saw it. What's important is that she said that your free-floating anxiety is leaking out your pores. She said you often cry and refuse affection."

"She wore my pecker to a frazzle. I had to buy steroid ointment."

"Dad, there are dozens of effective lubricants on the market. Just BUY some old-fashioned Corn Huskers."

"I don't need it anymore. I dropped her off in Malta, Montana, to be with her daughter and husband. I didn't bother telling you that Marybelle was a world-class fibber."

"She didn't mention she was married but that's beside the point. And by the way Mom wants you to talk to her. She's on the outs with Fred. She says he's a gold digger."

"Your mother divorced me in February. I'm not about to talk to her. She took my home and my livelihood. I don't care if that bitch drops dead."

"Let it all out, Dad. Give your feelings some OXYGEN."

I turned off the phone so he couldn't call back. I looked around the pumps at the gas station and wondered if I could work in one. My friend up near Pellston had offered me seven bucks an hour to work in his even though he owed us five grand but then maybe he had paid Vivian and she had pocketed the money without telling me.

I was headed west on 90 toward Seattle trying to figure out why there were these big round lumps out in the pastures. There were so many for so many miles that they had to be from geologic upheavals. This called to mind the idea that to live was to spend all day every day walking across a freshly plowed field. In short, lumpy. The trouble is that every single day you have to take your whole person along for the ride. There aren't too many clear victories that I can remember. A few weeks before Vivian's fateful meeting with Fred at the high school reunion on Mullett Lake I sat on the sofa with her trying to console another big butt depression. I made the obvious point that

her butt wasn't even in the top 50 percent up in our area.
I had recently run a bull I had sold over near Gaylord and
when I stopped at Burger King there was a long table of a
dozen middle-aged ladies all eating the same thing: two
Whoppers, fries, and a chocolate shake. The counter girl
told me that they met every Tuesday to discuss our many
"moral fiber issues." Anyway, I tried to tell Vivian that
scarcely anyone looks like the women in magazines, movies, and television. Sitting there on the sofa, however, I
realized my cause was lost. Vivian comes home all played
out from her real estate profession saying her "guts are in
a knot" from her work which isn't helped by Pepsi and
powdered donuts. At dinner she says it isn't fair that I can
eat like a "hog" and not gain weight because of farm work.
I remind her that when Robert was young and we worked
in our vegetable and flower gardens a couple of hours a
day she didn't gain any weight. She says, "Fuck you." Tears
fall. My special fried chicken gravy curdles. I recognize
that I can't compete with her magazines and her television,
not to speak of the excitement of her job, and the conspiracy novels she reads. I'm too ordinary and slow in her
speedy world. When I said about her favorite novels that
there didn't need to be a conspiracy, they own it all anyway, she said, what do you know of the world? Maybe she
was right, but then on the evening news they talk faster
and faster hoping that they'll find something to say while
I'm trapped back there inside Emerson's essays.

   I was plumb tired by five in the afternoon, patting the
seat beside me as if Lola or Marybelle were there. I stopped
at Moose Lake Motel and they were all booked up except

for a "Junior Suite" which had a balcony overlooking the lake. I stood there at the desk, my innards feeling quaky at the idea of spending a hundred twenty bucks for a night's lodging but then doubted that my parents in the land of the dead would be aware of the transaction. I sat on the balcony with a medium-sized drink watching boats with trolling fishermen putt-putt back and forth across the lake. I was thinking that Viv would have enjoyed my luxury accommodations. There was even a small refrigerator, a comforting idea though I had nothing to put in it. I checked the cell phone and there were seven messages from Marybelle, the last three from Billings from which I decided she was flying back to Minneapolis to see her friend in distress.

I wanted the whiskey to settle me down before I actually listened to the messages. On the balcony I felt like a missile or rocket without ground control. Up to this point I hadn't questioned the rightness of my trip but suddenly I wondered if I were truly suited for travel. Reality seemed to be crumbling and I was wise enough to understand that reality stayed the same so it was my mind that was crumbling. I wondered if I was coming down with one of those nervous breakdowns that seemed to hit Viv in the brainpan once a year. It was network news time but I stayed out on the balcony while thoughts putt-putted through my brain like the boats out on the lake. Early in our marriage we used to hold hands on the sofa while watching Walter Cronkite. Viv would sip at her butterscotch schnapps and say, "I wish Walter was my dad." Viv's real dad was all in all a complete asshole. When he died she didn't shed a lot

of tears. He was what you call a "blowhard," a real Sena-
tor Snort.

Maybe we were just another couple who faded late
in the game. I didn't offer her a lot in my back-to-nature
binge after I quit teaching. We English majors of a serious bent are susceptible to high ideals we paste on our lives
like decals. When we got married she pretended that as a
farm girl she loved nature but in fact she couldn't handle
mosquitoes, horseflies, blackflies, spiders, and snakes. The
only thing she really liked about Lola was that Lola would
kill and eat garter snakes in the yard. Lola asked for my
attentive affection a half dozen times a day, especially to
have her spine rubbed, also under her chin. Now on the
balcony it occurred to me that perhaps people should also
smooch that often. Was I designed to fly solo? Time would
tell. Right now I felt like a defunct species, an old
Studebaker sitting in the weeds.

I went down to the motel restaurant and ate two full
orders of delicious halibut the motel owner had recently
caught in Alaska. That brought up the problem of my ter-
minal fear of flying and how on my so-called tour of the
states I'd have to leave out Alaska and Hawaii. When I
reached San Francisco maybe I'd ask Robert to write up
those states since he had been to both in his movie location work.

Having finished my second order of halibut I felt tears
welling in my eyes at the memory of how much Lola loved
the skin of fried fish. And like the Indian waitress the serving woman was concerned about my tears. And again I said

that my dog had died. She said that she had been married three times and wished that her dogs lived longer than her husbands. I began to wonder what a sixty-year-old lost dog would be like. The waitress patted my head and I felt drawn to her though she was heftier than Viv. It was doubtless her human touch.

I returned to my balcony perch with a small glass of whiskey which I finally decided not to drink. Liquor doesn't work when you're feeling more than a bit flighty. All of these assaults on my sense of reality seemed to be coming home to roost. I always thought I'd be married to Viv until I died and in the last seven months I hadn't quite been able to rid myself of this thought.

To change my mental tune I played Marybelle's messages which varied from the first, "Keep your phone handy you wicked asshole," to the plaintive "I need you" from the Billings airport, to the final one from Minneapolis when she said that after she helped her friend she expected me to prepay a ticket for her to San Francisco when I was visiting my son Robert. This latter bit boggled me. I didn't think I wanted to see her again but then I didn't exactly want to be alone either. Farming had been pretty much a solo act and in decades of solitary thinking I can't say I came to any worthy conclusions.

I went to bed at ten and sure enough was wide awake at 4:00 a.m., early for chores if I had a barn. I headed west after figuring out my room coffeemaker, the pouch for which was on the short end for coffee. Crossing the Columbia River at dawn made me feel grand as the imponderable landscape, reason enough for this long drive. While at breakfast in Kittitas I studied the map, then headed south toward Yakima. After the soul-scorching traffic of Minneapolis I wanted to bypass both Seattle and Portland, Oregon.

OREGON

I was somewhat irked for unknown reasons to discover that
the jigsaw map color for Oregon was purple. Why? Perhaps
it was in the mind of the creator of the puzzle and forever
lost to the rest of us. Finally it dawned on me that the color
of the material in Martin's casket was purple satin. I had
been to the funerals of two friends about my age in the past
year which certainly destroys your equilibrium. Martin
taught history and hung in there until he had enough time
in to retire two years ago. The kids always referred to him
as Martin the Dork though he was somewhat revered as a
tough teacher. He always wore brown, smoked rum-soaked
Crook cigars, and when we went fishing I had to bait his
hook because he was squeamish about worms and minnows.
He couldn't stand our history after the Eisenhower presi-
dency and refused to teach it. He was a resolute bachelor
though he had an affair with a widow from Charlevoix,

Patsy. That was my other funeral. Patsy died of ovarian cancer in January and Martin gassed himself in his garage on April Fools' Day. I had thought he might choose suicide after Patsy died because he couldn't function without her. Martin was from a working-class family down in Flint and when he inherited a little money a few years back he and Patsy had toured battlefields in Europe. He took hundreds of photos that weren't too interesting to me though I indulged him. It's hard to stay interested in snapshots of Verdun and the Somme.

I found myself teary when I passed through Yakima. Martin was a specialist on everything awful that happened in human history and could pinpoint the locations on the world map. My American literature class came right after Martin's American history and the few brighter kids would come into my class quite disturbed, especially when Martin was teaching from the *Atlas of the North American Indian*. Martin was a map nut and believed you couldn't understand events unless you located them geographically.

When I reached Umatilla and tossed the Washington jigsaw piece into the Columbia River it occurred to me that in being upset about Martin I was also being upset about myself and my own age of sixty. My brain felt jiggly when I looked down at the river. Again, it was the sense of being without ground control. Viv was a bit paranoid and thought it was "others" who were in control but looking down at the broad powerful river I was on my own and my own trajectory certainly lacked the definition of riverbanks. A girl in a green skirt was leaning over a railing showing a lot of her brown legs and I felt uncomfortable because she was too

young, maybe fourteen, for me to be looking at. I turned
back to my car and felt further blurred by simple reality.
Jesus Christ, toughen up. That's what Dad would say,
"Toughen up." He would make up awful stories to prove a
point insisting that they were true. An example: "There was
a little ranch boy with a crippled foot. He left his muddy
boots outside and one morning when he slipped his crippled
foot into the boot a baby rattlesnake that crawled into the
boot during the night lay in wait. The boy's crippled foot
had to be amputated." This kind of tale was told to me when
I was upset over having broken the tip of my fly rod, or
sprained my ankle sliding into second base on the rocky field
we called a baseball diamond. The message was, bad things
can get worse and Dad thought this was very funny. Sure,
our little brother Teddy was a mongoloid but a few miles
down the road a farm family had a seven-year-old daughter
who was encephalitic and her head was so huge, bigger than
the biggest watermelon, that it had to be propped up by a
metal contraption at the county home. To my dad who was
a young man during the Great Depression the only truly
hopeless grievance was not to have a job, or not to have
"work" as he called it. This idea brought me back to Martin's
contention that Americans are somewhat unique in that a
smaller percentage of them are mere victims of historical
chance and circumstances. For most of us anyway there was
no overwhelming ground control that pushed us this way and
that. Back during the civil rights nightmare Dad had startled
me by saying that if he were a black man getting pushed
around he'd likely go to war against the whites. I was all for
Martin Luther King and Dad sounded like Malcolm X.

I got a little confused by my reverie. Here I was in north-central Oregon and I couldn't remember what Martin had had to say about the local Umatilla Indians. Something about them joining up with the Yakimas to go to war against the invading gold miners. Last night I had watched a few minutes of replayed Wimbledon from England before I slept and the babbling announcers kept talking about "unforced errors" and I was drawn to the idea. Here I was in very empty north-central Oregon where my own unforced errors played big from my brain's movie projector against the immense screen of landscape. I had been too damned wishy-washy. I had let my disgust with teaching ruin my love of literature. In college I had had a fine literature teacher, a Jewish fellow from Brooklyn, but then in college there were more proportionately intelligent students than I had had in high school. After class in college a group of us would follow this professor to his car in a remote parking lot hanging on his every word about Theodore Dreiser or John Dos Passos or Hart Crane or William Faulkner. I had lost my edge in my sentimentality about "the land" and I had finally lost Viv most probably because I had become a country bumpkin. Along came dashing Fred in his red sports car. So long, farmer.

I had become inattentive and missed a couple of preplanned turns in my route, then stopped at a gas station to ask about a scenic route. An old man, older than me, traced out roads that were remote enough to not be susceptible to cell phone calls. Mine had rung three times when I was still near Interstate 84 but I wasn't up to answering. Two of the calls were from Marybelle and the third was from Robert. Let them drift in the electronic void with their unspoken thoughts. I wanted to think through the idea that my college teacher had never for a moment lost enthusiasm for literature though he seemed to be the least popular man in the English department. On our last day of class he told us that no matter what we did for a living we should never absolve ourselves from being bipeds with brains. I had managed to do so, or at least tried pretty hard. Thoreau hadn't sauntered around like an eco-ninnie (AD's term) but had dwelt on profound thoughts. Over a year ago I had sat out in the calving shed next to a space heater because it was a cold March night and I was waiting for a cow I named Nancy to give birth. She usually needed some help and I sat there reading a little book called *Burnt House to Paw Paw* Robert had sent me. When Robert was a young boy we used to sit in a thicket next to the pond behind the barn and watch birds. Anyway, in this book the author is wandering around the Appalachians looking at birds and doing some solid thinking about life and art. I had snuffed out the dim bulb in the life of my mind pretending I was exclusively a Son of the Soil. For a change Nancy had a relatively easy birth. I only had to give a tug or two. Lola as usual went for the afterbirth and I had to limit her because it's too rich and I didn't want her to puke on her bed under the kitchen table. Believe it or not but Robert said he belonged to a group of gay bird-watchers in San Francisco. He said that once a month they get up as early as four a.m. and drive up to a place called Point Reyes. He's going to take me there for a picnic when I get to San Francisco.

I had thought Oregon would be as green as photos of Ireland but down near Kimberly it was dry and brown and

what they call high desert. I figured the green must be a
couple hundred miles to the west toward the Pacific Ocean.
What cattle I saw were a bit shy on weight unlike the plump
cows of Nebraska.

I pulled off the road and took a stroll up a hill in the
Ochoco National Forest. I didn't recognize the type of pine
I was walking through which were more sparsely needled
than the pines of Michigan. Looking upward at their
boughs I tripped and fell painfully forward on my chest,
my head narrowly missing a large rock. For unclear reasons I began laughing though it was an uncomfortable
laughter. I slowly rolled over feeling a sharp ache in my
left-side ribs. When I was a kid out in the woods I'd wave
my walking stick and say, "I'm the king of all I survey,"
doubtless got from a children's story. It was not exactly
original to have exhausted one form of life and to try to
turn to another. I had a sudden stroke of pure luck when
a yellow and black-headed Scott's oriole landed in a branch
of a pine directly above my head. We didn't have this oriole back in Michigan but I was familiar with it from my
third-grade Audubon cards. I stared up at this bird and it
stared back down at me. Parts of life are truly beautiful I
thought. Here I was flat on my back in an alien forest with
an intermittent throb in my ribs and along comes a bird
yellow as liquid sun to keep me company. Better yet, the
bird found me here and stopped to take a look. My friend
AD told me that in some primitive culture, I forget which,
the souls of stillborn or aborted babies are thought to re-
side in birds. I wondered where Lola's departed soul re-
sided. She knew enough not to bother porcupines because

when she was young she had gotten a few quills in her nose. However, she remained fascinated with them and would sit there under a tree and stare up at porcupines for hours. I discarded the porcupine as a home for Lola's soul and then decided the subject was beyond my ken. Life is clueless in such matters.

I hadn't moved except to breathe and now the oriole descended to a lower branch less than ten feet from my head. My heart had fluttered with its wings. I knew that they liked grapes and wondered if the buttons on my shirt resembled grapes to the bird. If I said hello the bird would flee. I decided I would hang in there as long as the bird and that the pleasant chore of waiting on the bird was as much as I could handle at the present time. Maybe our world had outdevised itself and only a few superior people could keep up with the world's speed. I was clearly not one of them. Now the oriole with its nearly garish color reminded me of when I was an agonized college sophomore thinking thoughts too heavy for my fragile head. For a brief month or so I came to know a poet-student my own age. He indulged my company at the coffeehouse because I was a good listener. He felt he was beyond hippieness as a lonely "space voyager through the history of world poetry." He was utterly threadbare and sometimes would draw a can of Franco-American spaghetti from his packsack and open it with his Swiss Army knife. He was reasonably good-looking and was often followed around by sorority girls. He mostly wore T-shirts and on all of them was printed in Spanish a line from a South American poet which translated meant, "On the day I was born God was sick."

Three ravens came over, spotted me, and gave their unusual noisy alarm. My oriole fled. I made my way down the hill to the car holding my tender chest. The "Fun Facts" that came with the puzzle said that Oregon was the beaver state, the bird the western meadowlark, and the flower the Oregon grape. The motto fascinated me: "Alis Volat Propiis" which means, "She Flies with Her Own Wings." That would be nice if it included men.

CALIFORNIA

Early in the evening I drove over the California border south of Klamath Falls but then turned around and drove back into Oregon thinking it wasn't fair to not have a night's sleep in Oregon. That's an even-minded liberal for you! It's hard with five weaned piglets because every single one except the inevitable runt will try to get more than their share of the food. It is apparently part of their nondemocratic nature. My friend AD says we should run a big pig trough through the main hall of the U.S. Congress. He even wrote a letter to the newspaper to say so and lost two out of three of his remaining Republican patients. The last of the faithful was a lumberman mogul's granddaughter who had come to despise all politicians. She had liked the older Bush but thought Junior to be "craven." She said this at the post office and a nearby schoolteacher had wondered what the word "craven" meant.

I was giddy after fifteen hours in the car and stumbled in a ditch when I stopped to take a photo of a group of late-spring Angus calves. There was still an ache in my chest from my previous fall and I thought here and there throughout the land older people are falling down. The calves only took nominal interest in me except for a single bull calf who snorted in playful anger. I had a sudden burst of memory of several springs ago when a dozen of my calves came down with common scours, luckily not bloody scours which is so often fatal. (Scours is a form of acute diarrhea.) I was up several nights with the calves and their concerned mothers. I had a cot with a sleeping bag in the barn so I wouldn't be disturbing Viv who could be a real bear when I inadvertently woke her. I lost one little girl and it was a sad late April dawn when I buried the poor soul out behind the corncrib. The burial mystified Lola.

I checked into a cheap motel just south of Klamath Falls to balance out my extravagance the night before in Moose Lake. I poured a small whiskey and pondered the meaning of the art reproduction of the sad-eyed donkey wearing a garland of flowers above the bed. Was this donkey print following me? I checked my cell phone. The ringer had been off all day long, a few bars of the *William Tell* Overture which I found irritating but had been selected by Marybelle back in Valentine, Nebraska. To show that life has balance the tiny window told me that there had been three calls each from Marybelle, Robert, and Viv of all people, the idea of the latter making my heart flutter despite my full swallow of whiskey. The calls were mixed in order of arrival. Robert was concerned about my "well-being." Marybelle was concerned

that I wouldn't "communicate" with her. Twice Vivian called
to say to call her back "immediately." Marybelle's second call
was to say that she was thinking of cutting off her hair because that was what her friend had done immediately before
being hospitalized in a mental facility. Robert called for the
date and approximate time of my arrival, then called again to
say that he had spoken to Marybelle about their mutual fears
and concerns about my mental well-being. Marybelle's third
call was demanding my estimated time of arrival in San Francisco. She also gave me the number of a Minneapolis travel
agent so I could call in a credit card number in order to prepay a ticket for her to San Francisco.

I was tempted to pour myself a second whiskey but
decided self-denial was in order. Somewhere in my weak
heart I hoped that Viv's third call would hold an ounce of
pleasant human sentiment. No such luck. Her voice was
brittle and instructed me to drive to Robert's with all possible speed and FedEx her power of attorney to clean up
some legal details remaining from our divorce. This seemed
a suspicious deal.

The phone thing was much worse than stepping on a
dog turd or fresh cow plot in the dark. On my way across
the parking lot of the motel to a diner for supper I envied
the first miners who were in the area a hundred and fifty
years ago without the convenience of a cell phone. Dad always inferred to me that he had a secret life in addition to
the one over which Mother stood as a domestic autocrat.
Dad certainly wouldn't own a cell phone which only made
the wandering man a target with the number providing a
guaranteed bull's-eye.

At the diner the meat loaf special was densely mediocre what with its ladle of generic gravy and instant mashed
potatoes and canned green beans. It was a supper that Lola
would have enjoyed. I was clearly losing weight far from my
own kitchen. I am an average cook but I work at it. Years
ago Viv said, "No more sex until you stop using oregano in
everything." Up until she got her real estate job Viv was a
tiger in the sack. She bought some mail-order nighties that
were real showstoppers.

I had ordered a piece of apple pie with scarcely any
apple slices in it, mostly glutinous filler. They have a lot of
apples out here in the northwest and I pondered why they
would cheapen up on the apple content. Searching for apple
bits in the filler that resembled cow snot I traced the ori-
gins of some of my unrest. I hummed a strain of the song
"California, Here I Come." It was always a common assump-
tion among us English majors that California was a bad place
and its effects on the life of the United State malodorous.
The entertainment industry was trashing the soul life of our
great nation. That sort of thing. Here I was on the verge of
entering the belly of this vast western beast.

More troubling was one of Robert's three phone messages where he had said Marybelle seemed to have "a good
head on her shoulders" and her multiple concerns for my
character were credible. Robert was always a language buff
and is doubtless a sucker for Marybelle who talks in para-
graphs on the phone. There was a sudden troubling thought
that nobody seems to know much of anything. Everything
in our culture seems to be marinating in the same plastic sack
and the ingredients are deeply suspect.

Before I slept under the stare of the flowery donkey I watched the big, fast girls in the Wimbledon tournament. Their Amazonian beauty gave me a nut tingle for Marybelle. Mother used to remind me to count my blessings and maybe it should have been "mixed blessings." I was nodding off when I thought with absolute delight that I wasn't worrying about my cherry crop. If it's not frost, or the rare possibility of hail which only hit me slightly in 1988 there are a bunch of things that can hurt you right now about two weeks before the crop is ready. High wind off Lake Michigan can bruise the fruit, say one of those black line squalls with wind around seventy miles per hour. The worst thing, though, is wet weather which is always possible up in our area which is well known among meteorologists for its major thunderstorms. Wet weather can bring on cherry leaf spot which has developed a resistance to the fungicides we spray. We had forty acres of tarts, and ten of sweets. If it's overwarm and wet your sweets can crack open just before harvest. I thought of going into apples for a while but too many farmers got into apples and there's an oversupply.

Shorn of the demanding farm, and heartwarmed by a Wimbledon Amazon howling in victory, I clicked off the television and fell into a deep sleep waking at 4:00 a.m. after a lurid sex dream of Viv at the height of her sexuality which was in her thirties and early forties before her real estate career kicked in. We were energetic lovers to say the least. I had an urge to call her but then it was only 7:00 a.m. in Michigan and she might be with her lover Fred. I felt a pang of jealousy, the all-time hopeless emotion. I fell into a doze for fifteen minutes but then recalled a silly dream I had back in college where I was told that I would become a jubilant man if I read page five hundred of a certain novel, but when I got to the library a hurried half hour later I discovered that the book had only three hundred pages.

I was back across the border into California at dawn with only the smallest trace of English-major foreboding. Northern California is an extraordinarily beautiful and varied landscape and is totally disassociated from the criminal mayhem on the Los Angeles–based television programs Viv favored wherein everyone is tough and full of smart talk and cars chase each other at incomprehensible speeds on crowded freeways. Of course the countryside way up north around our deer camp in the Upper Peninsula has no resemblance to Flint and Detroit. In these remote areas you lose the notion that America has worn itself out much in the manner that I have. How well I remember my Whitman-esque intoxication with spring on the beautifully landscaped university campus, with so many flowers that wouldn't grow in the colder regions of my northern homeland.

I had promised myself I'd be polite and return the calls to Marybelle, Robert, and Vivian at breakfast time (dry sausage patty and pale underfed eggs, but good fried new potatoes). I chose the easiest first, Robert, who didn't answer but I said I'd arrive by tomorrow afternoon which would give me the leisure to collect myself, and also drive west and see the Pacific Ocean. Viv sounded played out and melancholy. She didn't want to explain the need for my power of attorney and said the information was contained in an e-mail she had sent in care of Robert. Marybelle was a dissonant mud bath which was half-expected. She was back home in Morris and claimed that an old lover had showed up and had taken advantage of her sexually after she drank too much on a hot night. I didn't want to hear the details. She cried because the husband of her friend with the mental "crack-up" had forbid her to see his wife in the private asylum. When could she see me in San Francisco and when would I make sure that she got a ticket? I said "four days" wanting a little time alone with Robert.

Once more I had forgotten to throw away a puzzle piece and stopped near Little Cow Creek northwest of Redding, dropping Oregon in the water without emotion. I noted that California was known as the golden state and the bird was the California valley quail, the motto "Eureka" ("I Have Found It"), and the flower the California poppy. Except for the flower and bird it all seemed too much connected to money.

CALIFORNIA II

I cut due west out of Redding heading for the ocean through an area called Whiskeytown and observing that without Marybelle's presence I had dropped down to one drink a day and that to blunt my road frazzles. During the last week of our marriage when Viv was still present in the house we both drank too much. I'd say Viv drank at least half a fifth of butterscotch schnapps every evening and I'd do that amount of Canadian whiskey. It was real hard on Lola who since she was a pup could never bear a cross or raucous voice. Lola would head for a darkened back corner of the pump shed and stay there until we fell asleep. Once when Viv was carrying in groceries she had left her car door open and Lola got in there and ate the last five of Viv's package of powdered donuts. Viv screeched and Lola headed for the barn for three whole days and nights. My friend AD told me that people who gain a lot of weight fast always have a semisecret food vice and Viv's was powdered donuts and various kinds of soda pop.

We hit bottom the next to the last evening together when she said, "You just don't turn me on like Fred. You used to, Cliff, but you don't anymore." I saw red and threw a heavy oak chair through our picture window and then, since it was a cold windy night, I had to use duct tape and cardboard to patch the window. Viv helped hold the cardboard while I was taping and we actually laughed. The next day we were civil and hearing no human barking Lola emerged. This last day was especially hard because Viv was not a liberal democrat like myself and made no attempt at fairness while she was splitting up our mutual possessions. She even took a beautiful antique clock my mother's rich employers had given her and I had inherited. She said, "You'll never set this clock" which was true. During summer heat waves when we were sprinkling the yard so it wouldn't turn brown Viv made no attempt when moving the sprinkler to make sure each patch of yard got its fair share of water. Liberal democrats, like me, are careful about such things. When you're throwing out cracked corn to chickens and one is late arriving you throw an extra handful her way. When slopping the pigs I always made sure I carried my walking stick to do some gut poking to allow the runt to get a goodly share.

I had forgotten to turn off the phone and it rang from the backseat, five times to be exact. I wasn't tempted to slow down and grab for it. All of my life I have been willing to answer the phone but no longer. I had lost about half of my day-to-day ordinary mind with the divorce, and

now the other half appeared to be slipping away. For instance, the idea of changing the names of states and birds
had become very appealing. I also began to think about
God in particular ways. My mom had hauled me off to the
Lutheran church early every Sunday morning when I
wanted desperately to go fishing or even chop firewood
with my dad, or go visit a farmer friend of his who owned
a champion team of Belgian draft horses that always won
the pulling contest at the county fair. Dad said that these
horses were "the gods of their world." I wasn't sure what
that meant but it sounded grand. I loved to touch their
huge soft noses.

I stopped in Willow Creek for gas and made a halting
move toward the cell phone sitting there on the backseat,
cute as a fish liver. Marybelle said, "Cliff, will you ever learn
to answer the phone? The phone isn't a phone when you
don't answer it. Cliff, we don't have a future. I'll still come
to San Francisco. It would be nice to have a first-class ticket
because I've been claustrophobic and out of sorts. The president of a prominent American university once sent me a first-
class ticket from New York City to Miami. Anyway, I've
been brooding about our age difference . . ." the message
time ended and she called again. "Seventeen years is quite
a gap, Cliff. In ten years you'll be seventy and I'll have moved
from forty-three to fifty-three. I have to doubt that you'll
be sexually active . . ." End of message again. The third was
simple, "Cliff, just answer the fucking phone!"

I wasn't all that attentive because I was looking at a
motel across the road from the gas station. The magic was
that the motel advertised kitchenettes as many motels do

but it occurred to me that I might settle down in one for a few days and cook my own dinner. What I most sorely missed on the road was home-cooked food. Viv had been a passable cook before real estate overtook her life at which point I took over cooking dinner because she often wouldn't come home until seven. Frankly, I didn't start well but then saved my ass by following recipes to the letter at least the first time out of the chute. Now I terribly missed my chicken potpie, which was one of the dishes Robert had requested I cook in San Francisco along with meat loaf, spaghetti and meatballs, green chili stew, and a Southern fried chicken my friend AD had given me the recipe for after a trip to Louisiana for what he called "sexual therapy." Viv always liked food with hot chili peppers because she had grown up in northern Michigan at a time when the fruit crops demanded thousands of Mexican pickers and many of our local families had taken to Mexican food. Now with mechanical cherry pickers the Mexicans are largely gone and I miss them. When I was thirteen and picking cherries for money in July I saw a pretty Mexican girl emerging from a hedgerow pulling up her trousers after taking a pee. I instantly became so full of desire on seeing her little triangle of black hair I came close to fainting. Suddenly I'm not so sure that the Minneapolis prostitute was being truthful about AD. I've never known him to wear a hat except an orange stocking knit hat when deer hunting. Why would she make up such a story? I suspected prostitutes see some pretty weird behavior in our manly population. But peeing in hats? Such a request would be outlandish.

I was feeling pretty good as I neared Eureka on the coast. Here I was at age sixty and I was finally going to see the Pacific Ocean on a clear hot day. It came to me suddenly then that California should be called Pacifica and the lowly, common robin should be renamed a Rubens in honor of its fat round breast. I recalled that forty years before in a literature class my professor had as a guest his mentor from Harvard who had said, "In the realm of absolute imagination we remain young late in life." None of us youthful smart-asses put much stock in the statement at the time but I had hopes that here in the present it was true. The hugeness of the project boggled me. True, there were only fifty states that needed work, and I had forgotten how many kinds of birds we had in the United States but I seemed to remember it was around seven hundred. Rather than being merely adrift this was something I could get my teeth into. I could borrow western bird books from Robert or buy new ones. The states were easy what with my jigsaw puzzle in the backseat. I knew there was a trace of silliness in my intentions but my heart now felt airy with new oxygen rather than sodden with my difficulties.

The Pacific Ocean was more than I bargained for. At first I thought I might have a heart attack. Lord Byron said, "Roll on thou deep and dark blue ocean, roll." Well, of course. I spent the next day and a half between Eureka and San Francisco hugging the coast as closely as I could and stopping a couple of dozen times for yet another look. The ocean became the best smell of my life. I was generally astounded because nothing I had known or read prepared me for the Pacific Ocean. The tide pools among the rocks especially fascinated me. Thousands of wiggly-squigglies swimming around marooned by the tide. I began to think of the human race swimming around in an immense, cosmic tide pool. It was all a nonspecific religious experience. I sat on numerous beaches and stared at the ocean until it was ocean inside of my head. The experience was a world away from the American idea of God as someone who drove around in a dump truck full of figurative candy to toss to deserving people if you beckoned him properly. The ocean was a god unknown, galactic, and in her own quiet way maybe enjoyed the moon as much as we did, what with the way the ocean gets pushed around by the moon and her tidal energies.

I stopped at a motel for the night near Fort Bragg, a town that owned the tackiness of any locale with an armed service base but the difference was that Fort Bragg had the Pacific Ocean. I had a bang-up Mexican dinner which added happy sweat to my euphoria. Of course I knew I had become batty, perhaps deranged, but then I meant no harm to anyone or to myself. AD had said about my divorce, "The world is taking you to the cleaners and you don't seem to know it." That might be true but then I wasn't mentally equipped to stand and fight. Running for it turned out to be more pleasant. After the divorce was final in midwinter Robert had asked on the phone, "Would you ever take Mom back?" And I said, "Probably." Viv had never cared a hoot for big ideas, the life of the mind, or good literature, but then she was so much in the here and now she could draw me out of my deep streak of melancholy. In the past year since the ill-fated high school class reunion, life had utterly lost its predictability but then maybe predictability causes melancholia?

I was a little woozy from the three pokes of tequila and two Pacifico beers, my first Pacifico but what other beer could I order? I checked the cellular back in the room and then drove a few miles south to a place called Point Cabrillo to say good night to the ocean. The messages from Robert and Marybelle had expressed concern for my mental well-being and I wondered how this had all got started. Not since breaking my left arm in childhood had people needed to be concerned for me. I couldn't figure out what it meant other than human mischief originating with Marybelle though Robert has always needed something or someone to worry about. Marybelle had also made the slightest apology for her concern about our age differences and said, "There are miracle drugs that can keep a man active until he's a hundred." While looking at the Pacific I laughed imagining myself a wizened flying squirrel hurling myself on unsuspecting women while aiming my boner before I leapt.

When the sunset headed toward China I drove back to the room with a glad heart. I paused at a stoplight to toss a folded-up five-dollar bill to a scraggly young man holding a sign that said, "Will work for food." At base it seems that's what we all do. At dinner my ears had reddened watching a pretty Mexican waitress float across the room with her trays of food. There was Mexican music on the jukebox and I felt like I was in a foreign land, Mexico to be exact. The music and the ocean stayed with me all night when I awoke a dozen times still feeling good as Lola did when we did the morning chores. She'd prance half-sideways in a fancy gait on the way out to the barn.

CALIFORNIA III

I reached Sausalito at 4:00 p.m. figuring that I'd call Robert and then have a quick hamburger because Robert never
has dinner until eight in the evening by which time I'd be
half-batty with hunger. In between stints of driving I had
been walking beaches and had forgotten lunch within the
thrall of the sea. My longest hike had been at Point Reyes
where I had watched a group of evidently young seals
keeping an eye on me. I had dozed against a boulder during which time they had approached quite close. I said,
"Hello" softly, wondering if seal thinking and dreaming
wouldn't be totally absorbed in the oceanic rhythms I
found to be so soothing. I had read that sharks eat seals
but that wouldn't be all that bad compared to a prolonged
stay in an oncology ward.

I had just pulled off the freeway in Sausalito and was
near the former home of my boyhood hero Jack London

when Ron died. Ron is the private name of my thirteen-year-old Ford Taurus with just short of two hundred and fifty thousand miles on it. The actual Ron was a high school friend who died when his tractor (a John Deere) tipped over backward on top of him while he was pulling a stump. Ron was impetuous and had a heavy foot on the gas. He couldn't wait to graduate from high school and join the marines. He wanted to go to Vietnam and fight for our "freedom." By naming my Taurus after Ron I was honoring his hope-lessly swaggering memory. At his funeral at the Method-ist church Ron's uncle, also named Ron and an ex-marine, said that Ron would have made a great marine whatever that might mean.

Anyway, I coasted into a parking lot with a smok-ing Ron. Luckily a Mexican fellow was sitting on a phone truck drinking coffee and trotted over with a fire extinguisher. When I popped the hood the smoke bil-lowed out. I had blown a head gasket covering the whole engine with oil. The wiring had begun to burn and the Mexican hosed the engine down with foam before the flames could reach the carburetor which would have started a gas fire.

"Your car is shitcanned," the Mexican said. There was the name "Fred" on his shirt pocket.

"Thanks, Fred. I think my car has gone to heaven."

He laughed and walked back to his truck. This Fred made me think of Vivian's Fred but only for moments. I called Robert with the bad news and he said, "Good rid-dance" to Ron's demise, and then told me to walk a few blocks down the street to the No Name Bar. Robert had a

scheduled conference call with "Glitzville" and would send
someone to pick me up.

At the bar I had a whiskey and a wonderful ham and
swiss sandwich. One thing that has gone wrong in America
is the general acceptance of bad ham. The bartender wasn't
busy and we talked about Jack London. He was curious
about my strange accent and then said Jack London was
still real popular in Russia. I told him I had once started a
campfire under a snow-laden fir tree and sure enough the
snow fell off and doused the fire. It was a literary experi-
ment. The bartender was pleased with the story and said
literature can be dangerous and that when he was at Berke-
ley reading Dostoyevsky it sent him into a long depression.
I told him that my friend Doctor AD insisted that certain
books should have a product safety label pasted on their
covers. AD teases me that my early addiction to Emerson,
Thoreau, and Thomas Jefferson has made me too susceptible to contemporary bruising.

When I came out of the toilet the bartender said,
"Your driver is here, sir," and pointed at a young man in
a black suit near the front door. Vivian always loved movies about the high life where folks in fine clothes are
whisked here and there in a limousine by a chauffeur who
wears a jaunty cap. My driver's name was Ed and when
we walked out of the bar he pressed a button on his key
chain that started the big black shiny car, a BMW. While
we fetched my gear from the dead Taurus I found out that
Ed hailed from a farm town near Springfield, Missouri, and
had come west because he was interested in the theater. It
turned out my son Robert had gotten Ed the job as a driver

and that he frequently drove Robert to the airport. I naturally asked why Robert couldn't drive himself to the airport and Ed laughed in surprise saying that Robert sometimes dictated thirty e-mails to his secretary on the way to the airport and might also field a dozen or more cellular calls. I was thinking about this when a wrecker turned up to tow away my car, also summoned by Robert. I signed over the title and patted old Ron on the hood in good-bye. Naturally a car can't remember anything but it contained some fine memories. I stood there drifting away with a vision of Marybelle with her feet up on the dashboard revealing the wonderful undersides of her thighs and her possibly divine muffin. The Greeks had the Delphic Oracle but I forget what it said.

Robert's condo was way too spiffy for comfort. While Ed the driver put my stuff in a bedroom Robert waved lamely from the den where he was chattering on the phone. The whole place reminded me of a photo in one of Viv's *House and Garden*–type magazines. I selected three of Robert's bird books from a shelf and sat down on a sofa so soft that I feared I'd never be able to get up. I fell asleep looking at orioles. Was it fair that the west had more different orioles than east of the Mississippi?

"Poor old Dad, you look beat up," Robert said, waking me up.

"Oh bullshit. I'm fit as a fiddle." I didn't take offense because I had had a pleasant dream of Lola sitting beside me on the John Deere.

"Dad I was on the PHONE for three fucking hours.
I'm going to have a BIG martini. Do you want one?"

"Don't mind if I do." Robert was dressed as spiffy
as his living quarters and shook the martinis and ice over
his shoulder like they did in old movies. I went down the
hall to the toilet and on the wall there was a photo of a
black man with a big wanger by a photographer with the
nice name of Mapplethorpe. To tell the truth I looked
played out in the mirror but then I had driven about 2,500
miles in Ron before he died not to speak of my aerobics
with Marybelle.

Robert made us dinner on a stove about ten feet long.
The food was so good I became a little teary. Despite what
they say about the food revolution in America I saw little
proof on the road. He grilled a veal chop, and made some
spaghetti with just olive oil, garlic, and parmesan, and a
salad of dark bitter greens. I poured extra olive oil on
my noodles because it was so tasty and reflected that the
olive oil was from Italy and the wine from France and they
must have cost an arm and a leg but then Robert was forever a bachelor and didn't need to save up to put kids
through college.

We mostly talked about Viv and our destroyed marriage. Robert said that kids wanted their parents to stay
together no matter what and though he was no longer
a kid that didn't matter. We stayed up fairly late for
me, eleven o'clock, wrangling over the permutations of
the marriage. He wanted me to say that I would take
Viv back but I was unable to fully make that promise.

How could I become a houseboy for a busy realtor when I didn't have a farm? He put Spanish music on the record player and there was a beautiful song called "Beige Dolorosa" which I instantly recognized should be my new name for a bird known to others as the brown thrasher. When I went to bed Robert said, "Dad, Dad, Dad, I'm SURE Mother still loves you. She just has so many confusing issues." On my bed table there were the power-of-attorney papers and a FedEx self-addressed envelope from Vivian. Stuck to the papers was a note from Robert saying, "Dad, don't sign this."

I got up per usual at 5:30 a.m. which had become an issue in our marriage. Viv said my early waking hour disturbed her even though I slipped out of bed quietly and she never seemed to wake up. For the last years of our marriage I had been sleeping in a small spare room which allowed Lola to move out of the pump shed and join me with an air of victory. Viv didn't want me in Robert's old room which was more comfortable. He had been gone eighteen years but she kept the room just so for his yearly visits.

It took a while but I finally figured out Robert's hi-tech coffeemaker and took a cup out on a spacious balcony to watch the sunrise. As the sky lightened it occurred to me the sun was rising to the east behind me. I saw it glinting on the Golden Gate Bridge. When you're on the road it's hard to keep your directions straight. Newspapers every year or so will run a story on how many people jump off the Golden Gate Bridge and I hoped that no one would try it at the moment. It occurred to me that the stone surface might be a little heavy for a balcony but when I got down on my knees and scratched the surface with my penknife it turned out to be fake sandstone. You can't be too careful. I didn't quite realize I was singing which I always did on the tractor to pass the time and then I heard myself warbling a country ditty, "What's made Milwaukee famous has made a loser out of me."

"Dad, what the fuck are you singing at this hour?" Robert was behind me in an enormous fluffy robe.

I apologized but he said he had to get up within a half hour anyway. He had told me the evening before that he had to make a quick trip to Santa Barbara on a producer's private jet. A madcap period comedy was being made about three Republican wives in Reno waiting for their divorces. Two weeks into the shooting the producer decided that he wanted to move the production to British Columbia because of the enormous tax break the Canadians offered. Robert was flying to Santa Barbara to convince the producer that you couldn't "fake" Reno in British Columbia. Also, the director had threatened to quit.

Robert made me my favorite breakfast of sausage, fried eggs, and spuds while he ate a bran muffin and yogurt. Lola used to leave the room when Viv ate yogurt. Vivian would threaten Lola with a spoonful of yogurt and Lola would growl.

On the way out after giving me various instructions on how to get back in the condo when I took a walk, and where the stuff was for the dinner I was to cook (my patented spaghetti and meatballs), Robert dropped the startling news

that he would be picking Marybelle up at the airport on his
way home in the late afternoon. At the door he handed me
a letter Viv had written him to explain why she left me which
was a virtual car bomb in my heart.

CALIFORNIA IV

Where are the pieces of my heart this morning? I sat on
the balcony and read Vivian's letter several times. I had
Robert's bird-watching binoculars and between readings
I watched the great surging of the outgoing tide under the
bridge emptying part of the harbor and bay. I wanted to
be one of those miniature men in children's stories who
could ride away on a bird's back. Viv began with "Dearest Roberto" because when Robert was ten he decided he
was an orphan from a noble Italian family and demanded
to be called Roberto. Viv cooperated but I wouldn't under
the idea that it was already difficult to keep Robert in touch
with reality. Once at dinner Robert asked, "Dad, what is
this reality you keep talking about?" and I was at a loss
for words. Here it is:

Dearest Roberto,

You know I'm a phone person and it's real difficult to put my thoughts on paper as you asked. In a way my thoughts move too fast for paper. On the phone I gradually talk myself into what I mean. Just about everyone does this nowadays. I don't know a farm woman who can afford a pot to piss in who doesn't have a cell phone. Besides I was never good at writing. In college I would have flunked the freshman course Communication Skills without a lot of help from your dad. I always admired your dad's word power but in recent years he mostly mumbles. Roberto, small things in a marriage add up. He talked about the weather day and night until I wanted to hit him with an iron skillet. What is the weather anyway? When we made our annual trip down to Bahle's in Suttons Bay to buy some new duds he bought five copies of the same brown flannel shirt while I was down the street buying a cherry pie. Can you imagine this? He kept cooking me fattening meals though I begged him to stop though I admit part of the problem is Pepsi and powdered donuts. He thinks my real estate profession is what he calls a "boondoggle." He used to take a shower every day but in the past few years he would come in from the barn and say, "I didn't sweat today." He smelled to high heavens like the barn. For all I know he's been messing with this tramp waitress Babe who works in the diner. He no longer likes to polka

which used to mean a lot to our marriage. Several
times I caught him singing country songs to his mutt
Lola who didn't like me. I found a French porno
comic book in his pickup given to him by his friend
AD. He's been drinking a lot more than me. All of
this is why I turned to Fred for love. To be frank,
your dad bores the tits off me.

Love, Mom

To say I was floored was a euphemism. I kept thinking of that last Ali–Floyd Patterson fight where Patterson
was getting hit with over a hundred jabs a round. Was I
really this much of a nerd or dweeb, both terms the young
use to describe booger-picking nitwits? I left the condo in a
hurry, but pushed the wrong elevator button and got off in
the basement by mistake which dislocated me and I began
to sweat despite the coolness of the basement. It took forever for the elevator to return so that when I rushed out of
the building I was gasping for fresh air.

Well, I walked for three hours uphill and down which
is easy because San Francisco is built on many hills. My
hero Thoreau insisted that walking will get rid of what ails
you mentally and this is true but only up to a point. I tried
walking faster under the idea more is better but I felt Viv's
dagger in my side and slowed down. Chinatown was the
best diversion because I'd never seen anything like it in my
fairly long life. I was still wearing blinders like a draft horse
but the sights and smells worked their way into my brain.
I couldn't help but buy a tea-smoked duck leg. The pro-
prietor of the store was upset because I had tears in my

eyes so I said that my mother had died and he was sympathetic and patted my shoulders. Of course I wasn't lying
that she had died but that was fifteen years ago. Chinatown
made me think of what Robert said the night before to the
effect that I should go to a foreign country where I couldn't
comprehend newspapers and television and everything
would be new. I remonstrated by saying I couldn't get on
a plane but he said I could drive south to the Mexican
border of California or Arizona and take a bus. Robert said
I needed a new world to get rid of the old. I tried to say
"I'm fine" but he dismissed me saying that I took off on
my trip without my fishing equipment or bird books. I had
simply "flown the coop" like a crazy old rooster. He tried
to soothe my mind by saying that Viv had read too many
Barbara Cartland novels and that is why she ran off with
Fred whom she kept describing to Robert as "dashing," a
word not used up home.

Well, I took a break in a pretty little park up on top of
the hill. I sat on a bench and noted that I was surrounded
by three fancy hotels and a grand Episcopalian cathedral.
The area was clean as a whistle and there were flower beds
everywhere and in the middle of the park there was a foun-
tain with playful sculptures that from a distance looked like
they were molded on figures taken from children's stories.
I lit a cigarette and a passing lady looked at me as if I had a
dog turd in my mouth. Viv kept racing through my mind as
if she were wearing track shoes. It was plain from her letter
that she loathed me though her objections to my character
were surface complaints. That's where most people seem to
live, I thought. I was drawn to her at age nineteen because

she was big, luscious, and ordinary. As people used to say, she was full of vim and vigor and offered a good balance to my melancholy and brooding that seemed to be passed on by my mother. I also fell in love with Viv out of reaction to a pratfall I had had with a girl named Aster during my freshman year. I was sure that Aster wasn't her bona fide name when I had wandered into the art department building and met her when she was hanging one of her paintings that looked like a ball of spiderwebs. We stayed together pretty steady for a month but then she ditched me when she figured out that I didn't have the wherewithal to take her off to New York City where she wished to live in a garret and have an artistic life. She insisted that Michigan State was chock-full of philistines. In bed she was a wildcat and even made a lot of feline sounds because she said the cat was her guardian animal. She was tiny and lived in a tiny room where she cooked brown rice and vegetables on a hot plate. She said our relationship couldn't continue if I ate hamburgers. By contrast when I started courting Viv she would eat two cheeseburgers, fries, and a milkshake.

Suddenly there on the bench I recalled a poem I had heard Garrison Keillor read on *The Writer's Almanac* on NPR when I had passed through Montana. A poet by the name of Blumenthal said, "I am, at heart, a scared and simple man." Did that add up to what I was after reading Viv's letter three times? If I am this solitary life within my skin why can't I control the confusion of my thoughts? No one else can do it for me. This wasn't an original question but then I'm apparently not an original man.

I was about ready to head back to Robert's condo to start my spaghetti and meatballs when the cell phone buzzed in my pocket. I squinted at the screen like everyone does but wasn't up to answering. I waited a few minutes looking up at a beautiful cloud and then listened to Marybelle, "Cliff, I yearn for your company. I'm on the run at the Minneapolis airport. You might buy a few clothes because you look like a hick farmer. See you at dinnertime. Profound kisses." The idea that she yearned for me seemed a mixed blessing. I was aware that my best chinos which I was wearing were frayed at the cuff and that my scuffed shoes were a decade old so I window-shopped on the way home. Dad always said to me, "Don't mope," and I prayed to a god unknown while I bought shoes, two new shirts, a pair of black wool trousers, and a blue blazer, for the sum total of nine hundred dollars, about 1 percent of my net worth on this planet.

Walking down Polk Street it occurred to me I had left both the key for Robert's condo and the entrance combination code on a slip of paper on the kitchen counter. This was dollaring up as a mud-bath day. I was diverted by how many young men on Polk Street seemed to be "light in the loafers" as they say back home but then I figured that like farmers they feel more comfortable socializing with each other. When I found out about Robert so many years ago and went to see AD he said, "Everyone should be what they are." Vivian surprised me by saying, "I was never interested in being a grandma. There are too many grandmas." We talked a lot about this for weeks but then gave up. We even started joking a bit. I told Robert when he

came home for Christmas that I'd rather he be gay than a
Republican. He loved this.

I stood there staring at Robert's building wondering
what to do and then I remembered I had Ed's card and also
a cell phone in my pocket. "What a bright boy am I," I said
aloud. He had the combination and key to help Robert with
his luggage and sometimes to wake him up, or so he said.

"You're in luck. I'm on the Embarcadero. Also Robert called to say he bought you a barely used Tahoe off a
movie company that finished production. Madeleine Stowe
drove this car. Isn't that exciting? I'll pick it up in Paso
Robles tomorrow."

Another piece of luck is that Ed knew how to work the
radar range to thaw out the hamburger for the meatballs.
Things were looking up ever so slightly. Viv had insisted that
I stop using anchovies in my meatballs because she had to
meet the public in her job. "Just brush your teeth twice," I
had said. My dad loved garlic and anchovies and that's one
way I took after him. "Strong flavors for strong men," Dad
would say. Ed also pretended he admired my new clothes
though it was easy to see that they weren't of the high qual-
ity that he wore as a chauffeur. He left after opening me a
fine bottle of French wine. On the way out he did a little
dance and sang, "I got a date with a daydream."

CALIFORNIA V

With death we will become unknown to ourselves. Did I believe this thought? I couldn't say as I finished the spaghetti sauce and the bottle of French wine at the very same time which didn't quite restore my balance as it might have in the past. I studied the label of the bottle which read Domaine Tempier Bandol and despite the wine being red it tasted as if sunlight had been captured in the bottle. I lit a cigarette. Viv had helped me quit for twenty-five years but now living longer did not seem such an admirable motive. On the far end of the kitchen counter on top of a stack of Robert's mail there was an ad from a magazine called *The Economist* with this admonition, "Never lose your place in the world." Wouldn't it be nice to think so? It's not something you do on purpose.

I showered, shaved, put on my new clothes, and went out on the balcony and sat with the binoculars. For a country person the idea of people living and working in tall layers can be startling. My friend AD has a friend who lives on the ninetieth floor in Chicago. That's really up there. The building actually sways a bit in strong winds off Lake Michigan. AD told me this when we were driving back from Traverse City where we heard a speech by a prominent environmentalist who struck me as a nitwit. He rattled on in a rubbery voice about the methane gas emerging upward from cattle feed lots and the challenge of turning a nation of three hundred million people into vegans. The showstopper was an old Ojibway shaman who gave the benediction. I had met this man when I went over to Grandpa's with my dad way back in my teens. The shaman was jolly but scary back then and when I questioned Dad he said that this man was in close touch with all of the gods and spirits on earth who hide from us to survive. "We're a nation of spirit killers," Dad said. Anyway, after the environmental speech this old shaman with an ugly, booming voice held a cormorant in each hand with severely twisted beaks from agricultural pesticide runoff. He said that rivers and creeks were God's vessels and veins and the water was his precious blood. Lakes were where his blood rested from the continuing act of creation. It was a while before anyone in the audience could say a thing and these folks are real talkers. On the way back home was when AD spoke about people living in layers to save space. For a man of medical science AD can be a little goofy. On Sundays he walks in concentric circles way out in the woods.

I heard the door open and waited a minute before walking in from the balcony because I was glassing the big tidal thrust beneath the Golden Gate Bridge, not a good place for a rowboat. I was also thinking of the way Lola used to sit by the pond for hours waiting for me to throw a stick in the water so she could retrieve it. She couldn't do it by herself. Life is like that. The question for me as a geezer was do I need someone else along on this merry voyage?

When I walked into the living room their jaws actually dropped and I was startled but then I realized it was my new clothes.

"Jesus, Dad, you look like a golf pro," Robert said as Ed poured him a martini. Marybelle began to laugh. She was not quite as bald as a hornet from shearing her hair in sympathy for her nutcase friend.

"I wasn't sure it was you." She continued laughing.

Ed was setting the table for dinner and it occurred to me that he might be Robert's "significant other." He told me that he was taking a bus to Paso Robles early in the morning to pick up my car. I was reflecting on a possible need to flee as I heated up my meatballs and put noodles to boil. I allowed Robert a single premature meatball because he said, "I'm so hungry I could eat the ass out of a sow," a family saying that had passed down from my dad. Marybelle and Robert had been wrangling about "the theater," more especially about Ionesco, Genet, and a contemporary named Wilson. This theater wrangling was to continue through the evening until I was half-daft, all expressed in a kind of bitchy slang which I as a geezer couldn't totally comprehend. At one point Marybelle took me down the hall in front of the photo of the black guy with the big wanger and said, "Our love is doomed." I couldn't help but wordlessly agree. We embraced and when I put a hand on her pert butt my insides buzzed like a humming-bird. I'm so biological, I thought.

We ate dinner real fast and everyone became drowsy until Ed made a big pot of espresso and served peach ice cream. This brought Marybelle and Robert back to life in their theater talk. The only part interesting to me was when Robert began talking about the social implications of the arts and entertainment. He said that his mother Vivian had watched a thousand trashy movies and read a thousand trashy novels and her mind had become irreparably damaged. This was close to home for me because despite Viv's scathing letter about me I still felt poignant moments of loneliness for her.

I got up from the table and wandered into the den to survey Robert's library more closely. My new tentative plan on my road trip was to drive partial days, say get up at my usual 5:30 a.m., drive until early afternoon, take a motel nap, and then read books and work on my birds-and-states project. I liked the idea of tilling an untilled field. It seemed ironical that so many years ago I had lectured Robert on coming to terms with reality and now he was telling me that I had to "restructure" my own reality. This evening his own seemed questionable what with the movie project in shambles because the producer insisted that Reno could somehow be faked in British Columbia. It reminded me how I had lost my plum crop three years in a row to weather. We were too far north to raise plums. My motive was greed as plums were going for about fifty cents a pound.

I selected ten books and took them into the guest bed-room looking with fear at Marybelle's suitcase beside my

own. I realized that not very far back in my mind I was planning an early escape. I opened a volume of Emerson for ran-
dom wisdom but didn't get it. The very idea of self-reliance
seemed banal when you weren't sure who your self was.

When I went back to the table Marybelle was dozing
in her chair and Robert and Ed were planning on going
out to a club for a nightcap. Ed helped me haul Marybelle
down to the bedroom where we undressed her and tucked
her into bed.

"I've never undressed a woman before," Ed laughed.
"She certainly keeps herself in fine shape."

"So I noticed," I said. "She could fuck the balls off a
cast-iron monkey as we used to say."

Robert was boozy and maudlin when he said good-bye.
When we left the bedroom Ed had told me that they were
going dancing and I had said, "Why not?" At the door Robert said, "Dad, you are on a great adventure and have been
liberated to a new life." I couldn't help but agree.

I finally fell asleep to Marybelle's light snoring. There
was the not too comfortable feeling that in this condo I was
bedding down on the top layer of a five-layered cake. I
couldn't get rid of the idea that nature had had too much effect on my abilities to pan out in this world. I was an old
baloney bull who favored the far corner of the pasture where
it merged into the forty-acre woodlot. A baloney bull is one
that has outaged its effectiveness. You cart it into the slaugh-
terhouse where it's turned into low-rent cold cuts. When
fairly drunk on French wine AD had said the gods murder
us in hot blood not cold. He had just lost out in surgery on
a downstate hunter with a burst appendix. By the time the

man's drunk deer camp buddies had got him to emergency peritonitis had set in. When I first met AD twenty years back we started out with a modest quarrel. He perceived immediately that I was trying to live out an "ideal" which he called "literary." This pissed me off but then by breeding I had to be polite to the new doctor in town. Besides he was good-humored when he said, "Normal people don't try to be normal people, they're just hopelessly normal people." Maybe I had married Vivian as an ideal but that seemed not out of the ordinary.

Marybelle was crying at 4:00 a.m. which woke me up. She claimed that her pal in Minneapolis was due to have electroshock therapy. I calmed her down and we made love in the most restrained fashion ever and then she said that she was an orphan because her husband was going to divorce her. I doubted this and while I tried to prepare a response she fell back to sleep. Last evening when she was pie-eyed I sensed a vacuum to which I couldn't begin to offer anything substantial. By contrast when she and Robert were talking about the theater she was fully animated.

I went out to the balcony at dawn with coffee and stared at the fog furling through the landscape. I had taken out one of the books I had borrowed, Martha Foley's *Best American Short Stories*, but my hands felt too lame to open it when my own story seemed interminable. It occurred to me that like Marybelle I needed to pour myself into something with the same energy I had given to teaching and farming. My *self* obviously couldn't be a full-time profession. The birds and the states would have to do for the time being. I had swiped Robert's Sibley book on western birds and had my jigsaw of the states. What more did I need?

Lo and behold I fell asleep and woke up lucky at mid-morning. The upshot was that a friend of Ed's had driven him to Paso Robles in the middle of the night and Ed retrieved the Tahoe at dawn. Now he was in the kitchen having breakfast with Robert and Marybelle who were bent on going off to look at some office space for Robert who was feeling jammed at having an office at home. "Like your work shed, Dad," he said, and I felt lonesome for my shed with its woodstove, books, and a sheepskin cushion for Lola.

When Robert and Marybelle left I began packing which puzzled Ed who could barely keep his eyes open. He pointed out the gray Tahoe from the balcony and seemed drowsily concerned with my welfare. I explained I had changed my itinerary after looking at the Weather Channel and seeing that it was 107 degrees in Tucson, Arizona. I'd check it out but would likely leave the southern tier of states for the autumn. He wanted to know what to tell Robert and Marybelle and I said to just tell them I'd be back in nine days. When you're on the loose it's nice to be precise about something.

ARIZONA

Who am I that life disappoints me? I am embarrassed by this question. I can hear Dad bellowing, "Quit your goddamn moping." It seems like my parents die in my mind several times a week. Off they go in the monsoon of night birds flushing, say bullbats soaring around in the twilight. All in all Teddy was the happiest person I've ever known. He didn't have much in the way of language but he loved music. Mom would turn on the radio for classical music and Teddy would sing along to it in nonsense syllables. He was real partial to Mozart and would do crazy dances to Mozart around the kitchen and living room. I didn't start out liking birds but I sat on the sofa so often looking at the pictures in bird books with Teddy that I got to know these creatures. Sometimes if Teddy got to smelling a bit it was always because he had a dead bird in his pocket he'd found in the yard or back forty.

I was thinking these thoughts as I crossed the long lay-
ered bridge toward Oakland, the same bridge that had pan-
caked years ago in an earthquake. I was thinking that if
Teddy had the wherewithal to have a grand attitude toward
life why couldn't I have one? I had always felt guilty about
Teddy drowning despite the fact that I had tried so hard to
teach him how to swim in our farm pond. We had some carp
in the pond and Teddy always wanted to sink down and be
with the carp.

While thinking about Teddy I had taken the wrong highway. I was headed inland when I wanted to drive down the
coast. My brain made a satisfying split-second calculation and
I figured I could drive back by way of the coast after I saw
Arizona and possibly New Mexico and Mexico. Frankly I was
scared of the heat. Dad and Mom were both half-Swede and
Dad said his people had come from just north of the Arctic
Circle in reindeer country and that he also had a hard time
with hot weather. Viv loved the heat. She claimed it oiled her
joints but on the hottest afternoons I'd go back to the tiny
creek that ran through our woodlot and sit in a hole I had
dug out in the creek bottom. The creek was spring fed and
stayed much cooler than the pond behind the barn. Years ago
I read the Henry Miller novels *Tropic of Cancer* and *Sexus* sitting in the creek sipping at a six-pack of Pabst I kept stored
there. I couldn't read Miller back in college when everyone
else did for the odd reason that I saw a photo of Miller and
he looked a lot like my dad and I didn't want to think of my
recently dead father in terms of Miller's shenanigans.

Actually I had been hemmed in by traffic in my big
Tahoe and couldn't have made the right turn anyhow. I had

also switched on the air conditioner and couldn't figure out how to make it go off not wanting to take my eyes off the heavy traffic. I used to say to Viv, "Learn your car. Read the manual," but I never did myself. I could be a perfect prick in some ways. Now unless the traffic eased up the air conditioner was bound to freeze my ass. I used to save gists and piths on my long day's work on the farm and drop them on Viv when she got home from work. One day I dwelled on my favorite Jewish professor's lecture on D. H. Lawrence and when Viv got home, took a shower, poured a schnapps, put on her favorite Barry Manilow tape I quoted Lawrence, stating "The only aristocracy is consciousness" and Viv fairly shrieked, "What the fuck is that supposed to mean?"

I hoped to look up my old high school classmate Bert Larson who lived just west of Tucson. He had attended our ill-fated class reunion on Mullett Lake just to see if everyone turned out as badly as he expected, or so he said. When Vivian was so tardy in her return with Fred that day Bert had said, "Bivalves are always untrustworthy." He was so ornery in high school that he was hard to be friends with. He was actually "summer people" but at fourteen he had refused to go back to Ann Arbor with his parents who were famous botanists if professors can ever be said to be famous. He boarded with a widow and told me he screwed her every night. I never believed him because she was a Lutheran but maybe it was true. Bert wore a T-shirt that said "Resist Much." He went to Harvard but lasted less than a month. He took a bus from Boston to Tucson and enrolled in the University of Arizona because he wanted to be a student of desert flora and become what he called a "desert rat."

I called Bert from a rest stop near the city of Manteca, California, which I knew meant "lard" in Spanish. When young, say about twelve, I hankered to be a Mexican. At that age nothing seemed impossible. I was working full time on farms six days a week in the summer and was treated pretty much as an adult partly because I was a big kid. Bert's family had enough money so that Bert didn't have to work but out of contrariness he did anyway. On Saturday evenings we'd head down to the rural township hall where the Mexican workers would hold a dance with accordions and a few trumpets and a violin or two. We were shy and mostly stayed outside. They would set up grills and cook strips of meat and onions which you would eat in tortillas with peppery salsa. Bert had a mad crush on this lovely mostly blind girl about our age who sang with the bands. The next year she didn't come back north with her family and we found out she had died in a car wreck down in Texas. Bert was inconsolable though I knew he never had the courage to say a word to her. Love is like that when you're twelve. This girl was so good that she could sing perfectly without music. I thought of her over at Reed Point near the river when Marybelle was singing ancient songs.

Ed had showed me how to put the cell phone on buzzer so I didn't have to hear it ring. When I got to the motel in Kingman, Arizona, and took it out of my suitcase there were thirteen calls from Robert and Marybelle plus two from Vivian. I poured a smallish drink and went outside to feel the annoying heat, 105 degrees on a bank marquee. It's rare for me when the outside is hotter than my insides. There was a Mexican restaurant across the street with the positive sign of a full parking lot when it wasn't even six o'clock. I had this sudden good feeling that the life of the road might offer fresh thoughts in this extreme heat, the first of which was to go in my motel toilet, drop the cell phone into the toilet bowl and flush it. It was what Robert called a "great visual" to see the whirling, concentric current, and then the quiet quake and shimmer, and at the bottom the certain death of an electronic creature with nary a squeak. Sayonara motherfucker, as we used to say.

I had dropped the California piece of the jigsaw puzzle into the Colorado River thinking that a big state finds an appropriate grave in a big river. While finishing my modest drink I studied the map of Arizona which calls itself the Grand Canyon state, the cactus wren is the bird, the motto is "Ditat Deus" ("God Enriches"), and the flower is the saguaro which is a giant cactus. I didn't know a cactus was a flower but I suppose it is if they say so.

My chest and back still ached a bit from last week's fall and it reminded me of my youth when the two of us went on long hikes and I had to carry Teddy in a sling on my back like a papoose. He would roar off ahead into the woods but within an hour he'd get tired and I'd have to carry him home. By the time Teddy died he weighed at least a hundred so I was really getting my exercise.

After what I thought of as a fine Mexican dinner of the combination platter (one chile relleno, one chicken tostada, one cheese enchilada, rice, and refried beans) with a single Pacifico beer, and one shot of Herradura tequila (five dollars), I went back to my motel room and on impulse called AD. The conversation started out as pretty upsetting because it turned out that both Robert and Vivian had called him to see if he had heard from me.

"Do me a favor and tell them I'm fine. I'm not up to talking to them at present."

"So now I'm your errand boy? I'll do it if you deliver two cords of wood when you get back. I got this pancreas infection and I can't drink so I've been strip-searching my life. To be frank, it's no fun."

"I agree it's no fun. We're forced to look back because we can't see forward. Babe at the diner used to say, 'Different day, same shit.'"

"You have to forgive yourself for everything because no one else is going to."

"I have to ask you out of curiosity if you tried to get that party girl in Minneapolis to try to pee in your hat?"

"Well, like the late President Reagan I can't recollect that I did. I don't wear hats but that doesn't remove the possibility. I have to tell you that I saw Vivian in Petoskey and she said that if you come home she'll try to buy you a farm."

"She's the one who divorced me."

"I know that. I'm simply passing along the message. She knows from Robert that you had this young woman along for part of your trip. Maybe jealousy is making her reconsider her move."

"I have to clarify my thinking."

"That's impossible. You're trying to start a new life at age sixty which is also impossible. You can only try variations on your common theme. You're a raccoon who has been treed by the hounds of life."

"No, I'm not," I said and hung up the phone which in any form is a suspicious instrument except for ordering a pizza.

I was asleep at twilight after a pleasant sex fantasy about the woman who was the cashier at the Mexican restaurant. When I told her that the food was wonderful she beamed at me. Not many women beam. She was a tad hefty, maybe about 160 which was Viv's size, but this woman exuded mellowness and had the haunting scent of wildflowers. We shook hands and hers was moist and my groin was tickled.

I awoke at 4:00 a.m. and drank coffee waiting for daylight. I turned on CNN for a few minutes and there was a panel discussion about young people and drugs. I turned it off thinking that those blimpy little nitwits are on their own. I studied the road atlas and noted the Tonto Trail and Mogollon Plateau that Zane Grey had written about in the novels I once loved. The noble cowpokes pursued craven rascals and blackguards. I had recently read that Zane Grey himself wasn't too noble. Of course any English major knows that writers, perhaps because of their beleaguered early years, have nothing up on car salesmen, realtors, or grain dealers in terms of ethical behavior. I still remember the nasty March afternoon when a professor told us that Dostoyevsky had pawned his wife's wedding ring and run off to the Crimea with a thirteen-year-old girl.

ARIZONA II

When I was looking for Bert's place I momentarily regretted drowning my cell phone when I could have used it for
further instructions, but then I was inattentive at midmorning feeling a certain warmth for Viv despite her slander-
ous letter most of which was true. I had also been distracted
by the idea that I needed to get rid of all of these personal
"issues" (as Marybelle would have it) in order to proceed
with my sacred project of renaming the states and most of
the birds. For instance, I had no intention of changing the
name of the godwit. In addition I was having trouble con-
centrating because of the alien desert flora that surrounded
me. I had begun at dawn driving toward the fabled Flag-
staff then slowly descending five thousand feet in altitude
from the forests of the north to the hellhole of Phoenix,
then turning east toward Tucson. When I found Sandario
Road running through the border of the Saguaro National

Park I was stunned as if I had suddenly been transplanted to Mars. Finally I located the smallish dirt road that led to Bert's place with its hand-painted ominous sign, "No trespassing. Snake farm."

It was the strangest of days, already burning hot by late morning. Bert was out of sorts as usual and still wore a "Resist Much" T-shirt. Nothing should come as a surprise with Bert. There was a young woman named Sandra in her midtwenties wandering around humming but it was hard to tell her age because her face was leathery and her teeth bad, though her body fairly nice. These were telltale signs of meth intake, a longtime curse even in northern Michigan but only lately noticed by the authorities who still concentrate on the relatively harmless pot.

Bert showed me all the snake tracks in the sandy property and said vipers were hiding from the heat, adding that ground temperature reaches nearly 150 degrees, enough to start melting the sneakers of the woebegone wetbacks trying to enter our country for work. He ignored Sandra when she took a pee in plain sight near a cactus called a cholla. She was evidently a free spirit or a nitwit.

We ate a nice lunch of garden tomato sandwiches which made my soul quiver because it was my first summer in over thirty-five years without a garden and my very own tomatoes. Bert had heard from his old Lutheran widow friend, now in her eighties, that Vivian had divorced me. While we were drinking quarts of iced tea Bert advised me to stay away from women under the age of fifty because they speak a different language. The words are similar but the meaning is different from what it used to be. Across the table Sandra was petting a tiny rabbit who nibbled a piece of tomato on her plate.

By midafternoon the sun had become reddish from a distant sandstorm and Bert cursed because the monsoons were overdue. Bert left pans of water spread around the yard for the snakes but said they usually traveled to his pond way out back. People in the area would call Bert in alarm and he would remove the rattlers from their yards. He said that the roadrunner bird would eat baby snakes but not the big ones. We were at the kitchen table and now Sandra was licking the rabbit's face as if grooming it. The house was quite bare except for the living room with its walls of books and a desk.

We went out back and Bert began yelling and cussing. A neighbor's cows, mixed-breed Brahmans, had gotten through his fence and were standing in his tiny pond. There were several of them and their feet must have torn up the pond liner because the water was draining away and the fish that Bert said were tilapia were flopping around. Bert beat the cows with his cane and they ran for the back fence breaking it down. Sandra fetched a bushel basket and she and I waded in to gather the fish but we got stuck to midthigh in the mud. Bert went for his garden tractor and a rope and pulled us out. "There goes my fish crop," he said.

We walked back to the house and Sandra said her first sentence, "The fish will stink." Bert hosed us off and within fifteen minutes the first Chihuahuan ravens began to arrive. We sat under a tattered awning drinking cold beer and within an hour I counted seventy-three ravens out at the pond gobbling fish and screeching at each other.

Bert showed me to a spare room that had an old air conditioner in the window buzzing away. I was relieved because the thermometer on the porch said it was 110 degrees. It was siesta time but I had a hard time napping because of the strangeness of it all. I leafed through a picture book on cacti and watched the ravens out the window. They're a bit smaller than our northern ravens but behave the same. It occurred to me that Bert as an independent scientist rather than an academic one lived and acted more like an artist or poet. Such people came up to northern Michigan in the summer and the anthropologists and botanists were often as whacky as painters. While we were watching the ravens and drinking beer I complained about the heat. Bert sent Sandra for a map and he showed me a mountainous area near the Mexican border about seventy miles away that would be ten degrees cooler and I decided to head that way in the morning. I asked him why he was using a cane and he said that last year after he came home from our class reunion he had gotten nailed by a diamondback out by his mailbox. He had his own antivenom in the refrigerator but still lost a lot of flesh and the strength of his left calf.

I slept until early evening and when I came downstairs Bert heated up some coffee and set a bottle of tequila on the kitchen table. Bert was always handy at the stove and was stirring a pot of menudo which is tripe stew. We heard a pistol shot from upstairs and Bert yelled, "Sandra cut that shit out," adding to me Sandra was likely shooting at coyotes that were eating the rest of the fish out by the pond.

He told me that Sandra was from Uvalde, Texas, and was a bit gun happy. He had rescued her during a drug seizure outside the Hotel Congress in Tucson a few months ago and she showed no signs of leaving.

At dark Bert set up a spotlight and we sat on the porch watching the snakes glide around chasing rodentia. Sandra walked among the snakes but they were bent on rodentia and ignored her.

"You can't keep a dog or cat alive around here but Sandra thrives," Bert said, pushing a snake away from the bottom step of the porch with his cane. The snake struck the cane with a thunk and broke off one of its fangs, then crawled away with perhaps a toothache. I picked up the fang for a keepsake and when I turned I was alarmed to see Sandra take off all her clothes and flop into the hammock. She said, "Tequila," and Bert nodded so I went into the kitchen for the bottle, taking a gulp to calm my nerves. When I brought the bottle I looked away in modesty.

"A woman in a hammock is always faithful," said Bert. "It's a question of physics not morals."

The spot and porch light were catching Bert's face just so making him look older than he was, though I supposed this was partly due to nearly forty years of wandering in the desert. He had taught at the local university for a while but then had been "liberated" into being a private scholar by inheritance. It was then that I imagined that I probably also looked old to him. When you spend most of your lifetime outdoors you're not likely to look as smooth as a television newsman. A few years back Viv had bought me some

skin care products but I told her I couldn't go to the diner
for lunch smelling like a whorehouse. It was hard for me
to admit that I had started my little fandango with Babe
at the diner well before Vivian's downfall at the class reunion. One day after Babe's lunch shift she asked me to
fix the sink trap in her apartment upstairs. It took a full
hour and I was there on the kitchen floor yelling out that
she shouldn't pour bacon grease in her sink when I turned
around and there was Babe in a silly purple nightgown.
She put a furry slippered foot on my shoulder and said,
"Let's go for it, big boy." All those years of fidelity went
out the window. My friend AD said that marital fidelity is
part of the social contract and that the human mind is a
cesspool of errant sexuality. Any Lutheran knows what
Jimmy Carter meant when he talked about "lust in the
heart." Of course civilization would be destroyed if everyone simply followed the smallest cues of lust but then it's
also hard to imagine that the God of Abraham and Isaac
is keeping a weather eye on our genitals.

It was getting late. I helped Bert set up a fine-meshed
framed screen along the bottom steps of the porch so when
he got up at night he wouldn't be surprised by a snake crawling up the porch steps. Sandra had been singing nonsense
syllables in the fashion of my brother Teddy, then laughing, then drinking and crying. Finally she slept and Bert sent
me into his den to get a sheet off the cot. I covered her and
had thoughts about the wondrous physiology of women.

We tried to talk about Iraq but gave up with fatigue.
Bert thought that nearly everyone in politics was a chiseler
and I had had frequent bad thoughts about our boys being

sent over there with bad equipment that doesn't do what it's designed to do. What good is armor if you end up in pieces? We were practically dozing in our seats, and then Bert lifted his pant leg to scratch his wizened calf. We agreed that most politicians were the rattlesnakes of the human race and then we said good night.

ARIZONA III

Here I was at dawn on the Mexican border near a little village, really only four houses, called Lochiel where there was
an official customs crossing no longer in use. I shared the
stupendous view of a broad valley surrounded by mountains
with the rising sun which had a grander perspective but
mine was plenty good. Nothing can compete with the sun,
or so we were told by my second grade teacher who liked
to scare the shit out of us to keep classroom control. She said
that one day, perhaps soon, the sun would blow up and the
flames would devour the earth. We didn't always get top-
grade teachers at our little country school.

I stood there by the car wondering whether or not to take
along the war-surplus canteen Bert had given me. I had the
intuition that I should carry the canteen but then I had never
had an accurate intuition. Bert had wakened me at 3:00 a.m.
with coffee saying that it was time to get started. The upshot

is that a true desert rat does his exploring in the early morning hours before the summer heat comes on. He was pretty giddy because there was a chance the monsoons would begin that afternoon. We sat in his den drinking coffee and talking about the old days while watching the Weather Channel. He said he never slept for more than an hour at a time and that was why his sleeping cot was in the den next to all of his books. He walked me out to my car with a huge flashlight so I wouldn't get bitten by a rattler. We saw a couple with big lumps in their tummies from swallowing rats.

Meanwhile on the border my insides were tickled pink by gazing into a foreign country. I set off walking east along the border fence delighted with the strange bird calls and the sounds in my memory of the singing of the blind Mexican girl who was Bert's first love. When she would do the "coocoocooroo" part of "La Paloma" Bert and I would shiver. I also remember that way back in college when I looked at the map of Mexico I was thrilled at the idea there was a close-by country far from the banal torments of being an English major and where I wouldn't have to spend the entirety of a beautiful October walk trying to read Edmund Spenser's endless *The Faerie Queene*.

I was so excited by where I was that I walked too fast for an hour or so and when I slowed down my legs felt a bit wobbly. Act your age, I thought. In the distance, perhaps a half mile or so, I saw a dozen people scurrying along the edge of a beige mesa then descend into a wooded gully. They were doubtless migrants from the south looking for better wages. The floor of the valley was rolling grasslands but a little higher in elevation where I was walking there were patches

of oak and juniper. I knew from my map work with Bert
that the mountains to the east were called the Huachucas
and though they looked close enough it was an illusion and
I wouldn't be able to reach them.

After I had walked a full two hours I sat down under
an oak for a breather. Two hours out and two hours back
would about be my limit. It was half past eight in the morning and already getting warm. Sad to say after having one
of the nicest cigarettes of my life I fell asleep and didn't wake
up until ten when it was really getting warm. I was parched
but had left the canteen back in the car. Oh well. I was only
fifteen feet from Mexico which was across a few strands of
loose and rusty barbed wire. I crawled through the fence
so I could say to myself I had been in Mexico. I stood up
and did a little fandango, really a few polka steps, and slipped
back under the fence into the United States easy as pie.

I headed back west at a slow pace to conserve my waning strength. I should have had a proper breakfast, plus
weeks of driving had weakened my legs. At my age you have
to walk an hour every day to keep in tune. Suddenly a green
and white Border Patrol SUV came over a hill and jounced
toward me at top speed. I put my hands straight above my
head in the universal sign of surrender. A uniformed young
man jumped out of the vehicle, his holster unsnapped but
he didn't draw.

"I was watching through binoculars. What were you
doing back there?"

"I was doing a little midmorning dance." I couldn't
think of what else to say. He didn't seem sure of what his
next move should be. He actually sighed.

"You committed a felony by illegally entering Mexico and another felony by illegally entering the United States. I need to see your identification, sir."

"How am I supposed to know where Mexico is?" I asked, handing him my Michigan driver's license.

"Assholes take down the signs." He turned back to his vehicle where his radio was squawking. He leaned into the car and talked into a microphone but I couldn't hear what he was saying. He tossed me my license and took off at top speed. He was already a quarter of a mile away before it occurred to me that I should have asked him for a drink of water.

I walked another half hour until I felt dizzy and as if my legs were made out of sponge. I would have paid top dollar for a sip of water. Now it was hotter than a two-peckered goat and I sat under a mesquite and wondered if I was going to make it. Cliff, I thought, you got your ass in a sling. All of those beers and tequila I drank with Bert were coming home to roost. I touched my tongue and it was dry as dust. I realized I had been hearing a distant sound from the gray mountains to the south in Mexico, sort of like artillery fire in a war movie, but had been too worried about my thirst and weakness to dwell on the noise. Now it was louder and I swiveled my ass around the mesquite until I was staring at the mountains. They seemed to be getting bigger and I perceived through my blurred vision that there were dark clouds emerging that were the same color as the mountains, and also some enormous lightning strikes. The storm was still maybe fifteen miles to the south and I began to pray that it wouldn't move in the wrong direction. Wherever else I looked the heat was shimmering above the ground so that the actuality of the landscape wavered. I began to doze but then sensed that something was looking at me. I opened my eyes a wee crack and there was a roadrunner about fifteen feet away giving me a goofy look over. I had seen one behind Bert's place but it was racing through the desert a hundred feet away. I felt lucky that this one was so close. I had read in bird books that the roadrunner was the largest member of the cuckoo family. Its name was one I would leave untouched in my project just as I would leave alone godwit, avocet, and phalarope. It would no longer be "Wilson's phalarope" because birds shouldn't suffer the indignity of being named after people. I wanted to say hello to the roadrunner but I didn't want to scare him or her and anyway my mouth was too dry to talk. The bird approached within two yards of my outstretched feet and it occurred to me that she might think I'm dead. I had decided she was a female. Absurdly enough I remembered that I had read about a one-ton bird that lived far back in prehistory. That would be about the weight of an old-style Volkswagen. It would have been nice to see one. It was said that the bird couldn't fly. I imagined chasing one over hill and dale like trying to catch a draft horse, or perhaps it would chase me. I thought that maybe this roadrunner had come across a Mexican dead of thirst. Bert had said hundreds of them died of thirst in the summer heat and on my hike I noticed many empty plastic cartons they used to carry water. Now the roadrunner crouched down like a nesting chicken which made me sure that it thought I was dead.

I fell asleep and awoke in an hour by my pocket watch
to ripping thunder. It crackled and tore through the sky
about a mile south of me and there were lightning bolts in
the black sky that looked like maps of river systems with
splintery little creeks coming out from the main bolts. It was
preposterously beautiful in contrast to a nightmare I had just
had about Vivian and her friends having one of their canasta
parties where they would sing along to very loud Broadway
songs. It was karaoke straight from hell. I'd go out to my
shed workshop with Lola and turn on the radio.

Suddenly I saw sheets of rain headed toward me and
my brain yelled "Praise God." The rain hit me as if I had
been slapped by a wet towel. I opened my mouth wide like
a bullbat does for insects. I made a cup of my hands and
licked at the gathering water and then took off my shoes so
that they would catch the rain which they quickly did in the
cloudburst which was so strong I had to close my eyes. The
temperature dropped from well over a hundred to the coolish seventies. I gulped at my bad-tasting shoe water and then
headed west toward the car with my head down but I could
follow the fence. After about a half hour the storm passed,
and the sun came out, but I could see another was headed
my way from the southwest. My shirt was barely dry across
my back when I could see my car in the distance. Never
had a car looked beautiful to me but it did now. The world
had become too vivid and I decided that rain was the best-
smelling thing on earth.

It was twenty miles or so north to the village of Patagonia
where I had turned off the highway before dawn but it took
well over an hour to get there. I put the Tahoe in low-range

four-wheel drive and moved along the muddy road barely
making it over the steep hill out of the valley, and then there
was enough gravel so I could get better traction.

When I reached Patagonia I went into a Mexican restaurant and drank a lemonade and two iced teas. The water
in the canteen I had left in the car had become hot from sitting there but it had been far better than nothing. My dry-
ing clothes were crispy from the sweat off my body. The big
waitress had said, "You look like shit," and laughed. At that
moment I knew I had truly survived my stupidity because
she looked pretty sexy. I ate two full orders of enchiladas
and then checked into the motel across the street. There was
a wide grassy area in the middle of town and the motel clerk
told me it was where they used to pen cattle to ship by railroad. Cowboys drove thousands of cattle over the mountains from the valley where I had walked that morning.

I had a three-hour nap and when I awoke and took a
shower it seemed I had never felt better in my life. I went
down to the bar in the downstairs of the motel and had a
cup of coffee, and then a couple of drinks with four fellows
about my age who were talking about how hard it was to
live in short-funded retirement. I went out to the car and
got my road atlas and they showed me some nifty places to
see in New Mexico. Some young people came in the bar and
played the jukebox too loud so we walked down the twilit
street to another tavern called the Wagon Wheel. My companions were wrangling about birds, more especially the
bullbats that were sweeping around above us. Some places
they are called nightjars and down here a few locals call them
"goatsuckers" as they are thought to steal milk from goats.

One of my companions who described himself as a "failed writer" told me that in Kentucky authorities had found in the journal of a schizophrenic who had escaped an asylum the following quote, "Birds are holes in heaven through which a man may pass." This dumbfounded me and I hit the sack at ten a little groggy thinking about the quote.

NEW MEXICO

I left Patagonia at dawn with a glad heart after the same wretched cup of motel room coffee that had been following me around the country. Coffee requires coffee in it. I was just cresting the hill on the road to Sonoita, blinking my eyes at the wonder of the rising sun, when I swerved to avoid a run-over dog on the road. My heart sped up as I slowed down and then backed up on the shoulder to drag the dog off into a ditch. I've done this for roadkill for years not wanting them to end their existence squashed on the cement or blacktop. I got out only to discover it was a young coyote with his back twisted mortally askew. His eyes barely flickered so I stepped down hard on his neck to send him into the next world just as I would wish to be helped along if I were in that shape. Probably because of childhood books I've always thought of other creatures as our brothers and sisters. When Lola died the sobs that emerged from behind my sternum expelled themselves properly as a bark. My friend AD who has always had a half-dozen dog pound mutts running around his house said that dogs and young children always die with a quizzical glance. Being a doctor he should know.

I stopped in Tombstone, the scene of gunfighter mayhem, for breakfast. Given the right tools men will always murder each other. There was a young, alternative-lifestyle couple seated at the table next to me sniping at each other as they finished their cereal. The young man wore a blue-fringed leather shirt and had a gold ring in his nose. The girl was a little mousey in shorts and a T-shirt that chastely read, "Fuck Republicans."

"When I woke up this morning I began to think of myself as a Zen Indian," he said.

"That's a pretty big mouthful to chew, Danny boy."

"Hey, fuck you," he said, and walked out. She winked at me and paid the bill. To be frank, she had a perfect fanny which that fungoid nitwit didn't deserve.

When I started the Tahoe the buzzing began again which it had three times between Patagonia and Tombstone from a row of buttons above the windshield. It was a gizmo called OnStar which I knew was a kind of phone but I assumed someone was calling the previous owner. Ed, Robert's friend and driver, had told me that if I wanted to use it I had to call a number in New Jersey and have it "activated" which I had no intention of doing. I gave up and pressed a likely button.

"This is Jack Kerouac," I said.

"Dad, that's not funny," Robert fairly shouted. "What did you DO to your cell phone?"

"I drowned it in a toilet. It was abusive."

"Dad, you're a runaway! Mom is sick, sick, sick. She has Type Two diabetes. You should go home and HELP her."

"Robert, your mother pitched me out on my ear. Three of the eight friends of mine at deer camp have Type Two diabetes. What it means is they take a pill and can't have pop, desserts, pasta, potatoes, and bread among other things. Vivian is going to have to give up her Pepsis, donuts, and butterscotch schnapps for starters."

"Well, at least call her. It would be an ordinary act of kindness. She told me she NEEDS you."

Suddenly Marybelle was on the phone and her voice wasn't exactly Mozart to my ears. While I waited for the coming attack I watched five Japanese men dressed to the hilt as cowboys get out of an SUV and enter the restaurant.

"Cliff, I think it's time you reached out for maturity. You told me that you did the cooking in your family and it's obvious you're the cause of your wife's diabetes."

"It was Pepsi, powdered donuts, and butterscotch schnapps," I interrupted. "Also the occasional Oreo binge, as many as fifteen at once."

"Be that as it may who else could be at fault?"

"Vivian?" I suggested.

"Oh bullshit, Cliff. You're in denial. Meanwhile I think I'm going to start working for Robert in September as his aide, his girl Friday. San Francisco is seething with theater groups and I think I could return to the real me out here."

"What have you been all your life?" I was seriously interested.

"Fuck you, Cliff. What I want you to do is to come back to San Francisco and that way I could ride with you as far as Minnesota. I need to go home and pack up and that way we could talk about all of our issues. Frankly, I'm a little lonely for your dick, Cliff."

"I can't come back to San Francisco. I'm headed for Reed Point in Montana, that place on the river where you sang to me when I was sick. I'm going to rent a cabin, go fishing, and work on my states-and-birds project. It needs closure." I thought it might help if I used the word "closure," one of Marybelle's favorite words.

"Cliff, I need you. Just get here ASAP. Robert wants to say something."

I quickly hung up and then pressed buttons until I reached OnStar headquarters and talked to a nice-sounding woman who after a delay told me that my service had only been activated that morning and since the vehicle was owned by Robert he would have to "authorize deactivation." I gave up in a trance over her melodious voice. There was the idea that I could buy a squirt gun and keep shooting at the gizmo until it expired.

Lucky for me I drove off on a side road that had been marked on my map by one of the fellows in the bar in Patagonia. I was headed for New Mexico which is purple on the jigsaw puzzle. It's known as the land of enchantment, a feeling I could use. My friend the road-runner is the bird, the yucca the flower, and "Crescit Eundo" ("It Grows as It Goes") the state motto. I can't say I understand the latter and struggled to get my mind to let it pass.

I impulsively called AD since it was Saturday and I knew he'd be home before making hospital visits. He gave the alarming news that my grandpa's old place had half burned down because a yuppie had tried to do his own rewiring. It was for sale at a bargain price and he suggested that I try to get Vivian to buy it for me. This was a startling idea and I let it pass without comment since I'm a slow study. He then said that Vivian's prognosis was good as long as she strictly followed a diabetic regime. He was trying to clear a week to go trout fishing and we made some tentative plans to meet in Montana. When I pressed the button to turn off the phone I was a little alarmed at how suddenly the possibilities of life could change with a phone call. It was melancholic to think how badly my dad had wanted to buy Grandpa's place that had to be sold when the old boy got cancer. He had no insurance and the money had been eaten up in the usual unsuccessful attempt to treat liver cancer. My friend AD told me that it was not infrequent to see the aged devour their net worth in a forlorn attempt to stay alive.

My glum thoughts quickly dissipated in the beauty of the mountain landscape. My newfound cronies back in Patagonia had directed me on a challenging mountain route that would arrive at the location of Geronimo's surrender at the foot of Skeleton Canyon. I had remembered dwelling on a photo of Geronimo in a history book and thinking that he was the toughest-looking hombre in the world.

The road was a bit slippery from the recent monsoon so I drove slowly in four-wheel drive, pausing to check a set of large feline tracks crossing the dirt road that signaled the recent passing of a mountain lion. I beeped the horn at a group of skinny cows who charged off into the brush. It turned out it was harder to descend then ascend, and on the far side of the mountain I went into a barely controllable skid that made me sweat. I thought once again that we who hail from east of the Mississippi are rarely aware of how much emptiness there is in the west. At times it seems a little threatening.

When I reached Skeleton Canyon I decided to call Vivian. At first she sounded a little blurred and plaintive but then recovered her old Viv spirit the moment I tried to make a deal. I said that I'd come home if she'd buy me my grandpa's old place and pay for the cost of rebuilding it. I should have known this was the area of her expertise. She said she'd think about it though she would retain the deed in her name and limit me to a life lease. Love is like that. She said that Fred had tried to forge a check of hers and she was pressing charges. "Life without donuts is real tough," she said. She meandered about the hot weather, her horrid diet, and that she was thinking about buying a corgi pup. She found it puzzling that she could still love an old fool like myself.

I took a long hike up the road in the gathering heat, then drove up to Portal, Arizona, and checked into a motel early because I wanted to think things over. Life had gone from slow to too fast. At lunch (a green chili cheeseburger that made me sweat) an ancient waitress told me that Nabokov used to hang around Portal to chase butterflies. This was more thrilling to me than the idea that my own home ground once had Hemingway as a summer visitor. Viv even bought a table and chairs from a furniture company's Hemingway Collection.

UTAH

Nothing on my trip thus far was as I expected which shows you that rather than simply read about the United States you have to log the journey. I mean the look and feel of it. I've read that television has made us all the same but I haven't seen the evidence for that point of view.

Suddenly while traversing a mountain valley I felt a surge of resentment over the numberless times I had to teach Carl Sandburg, Stephen Vincent Benét, Edward Arlington Robinson, and Robert Frost. I mean they're all okay but then the repetition became sodden and I came to favor Edna St. Vincent Millay whom I read in college always while drinking two beers to help me feel her extreme emotions. The Frost represented in high school anthologies reminded me overmuch of my mom's weekly letters while I was in college so full of cryptic reminders of my "duties" which were never spelled out. She also liked to say that my dead father would wish me to be a "success" when my dad never spoke about such things except to say that successful people never had much time for important things like hunting, fishing, drinking, and wandering around in the woods. High school literary anthologies always seemed skewed to the middle path of good citizenship which means they left out the best work. In the middle of these muddled thoughts I stopped and tossed New Mexico into a roadside mud puddle around which Nabokovian butterflies fluttered.

In the midafternoon I was cutting across the Navajo reservation from Window Rock in the east toward the west when I was nailed by Vivian on the OnStar. She said she would put a down payment on Grandpa's place if I'd head straight home. I said "nothing doing" because I was aiming at catching some brown trout and meeting AD in Montana. She was pissed off and then teary saying that Fred was trying to jump-start their affair again. "He only listens to his own mind. He can't hear anyone else," she said, and then hung up on me. This comment actually reminded me of Viv at her worst. For instance, she doesn't want the cosmos to be so large. The night we returned from our last polka party we were standing out in the backyard and the stars were especially brilliant and I mentioned that I had read that astronomers had discovered that there weren't twelve billion galaxies, there were ninety billion. She was quiet for a moment and then whispered, "That's how much money Bill Gates has." Since I can't get my head around large sums of money I said, "I'm talking about galaxies," and she said, "I don't believe a goddamn word you say, Cliff." She went into the house leaving the odor of butterscotch schnapps in the night air. I had hoped we would make love but then I shot off my mouth about galaxies even though I knew Viv preferred earth as a limited homeland. With Viv gone Lola approached and I sat in the grass petting her while we listened to a couple of whip-poor-wills from out by the pond.

Viv's call made me lose my energy and I turned north toward Chinle. The air conditioner was on but the thermometer built into the rearview mirror read one hundred. I simply had to get out of this fearsome heat where even nighttime was as warm as a warm day back home. I fantasized about a cabin in Montana where I'd sit buck naked out on a porch at midnight and get real cold. This fantasy changed when I checked into the Thunderbird Lodge in Chinle and the clerk at the desk was a lovely Navajo woman who quickly joined me on my dream porch in Montana. She, however, was all business and evinced no interest in a white geezer other than to book me on a guided evening trip into Canyon de Chelly assuming no monsoon rains hit between now and then.

In my room I studied the road atlas for the route over toward Colorado City which had been much in the news because of apostate Mormon polygamy mayhem. When I first heard this news I tried to imagine what it would be like to be married to seven versions of Vivian. Better to volunteer for the front lines in Iraq or Afghanistan. Now in the room I remembered that I first noticed Viv when she was running the bases for the girls' softball team. She bowled over the Boyne City shortstop and second baseman. I was a timid soul at the time and she was a little hefty for my taste but I wholeheartedly admired her boldness and verve. Throughout our marriage when there was an illness or death or injury in our country neighborhood Viv was always the first one there to help out by organizing everything. When our neighbor Durwood lost a hand to a faulty corn picker Viv got him a hotshot lawyer in Suttons Bay and now Durwood and his wife tour the south every winter in their fancy motor home. Everyone describes Viv as a "go-getter." This certainly did not mean that Viv would be sympathetic to my project which now seemed part of my destiny, a big word but what else could I call it? I'd have to keep it hidden from her just as my college heroine Emily Dickinson kept her poetry writing largely a secret. When she finally showed her verses to the eminent editor Higginson he turned out to be largely a nitwit.

I fell asleep and missed my tour of Canyon de Chelly thus losing my thirty-dollar deposit. So it goes. I had become self-indulgent and careless. Thirty bucks was a day's work in the former times but when I took a stroll there was an explosive cloud burst and the tour dune buggies came racing in with drenched passengers. I stood there in the parking lot in the sheets of rain taking an alfresco shower, not wanting anything else on earth except to be cold and wet, smelling the heat disappear from the rocky landscape into the rich odor of rain.

I had a gorgeous dinner of chile rellenos at the lodge, hot peppers stuffed with meat and cheese. The Navajo Nation is dry and I had run out of whiskey which seemed to make my dreams more vivid. My dreams kept returning to images from a childhood book, *Brave Tales of Real Dogs*. My mother didn't care for dogs so Dad read it to me. It was easy enough back then, and occasionally now, to wish to be a dog running through the mountains, perhaps with a flask of precious serum tied around its neck to save a remote and imperiled village. However, in my confused dream my run through the Alps had been accompanied by small elephants obviously leftover from Hannibal's trek, another favorite story of my dad's.

These images did not permit sound sleep and I awoke at 4:00 a.m., turned on the light, and discovered a dead fly in my bed. Maybe I rolled over on it, poor thing. It owned a leg and head like me. Luckily I had bought extra coffee packs at a convenience store and made a strong little pot. In my run across the Alps as a dog there had also been flocks of birds in the pink, twilit sky. Anyone who has picked up a dead blackbird knows that it's not truly black. In a notepad next to the desk phone I wrote down "darkbird." Not great but not bad. I had no fear of avian flu thinking the scare similar to Viv's frenzy over the Y2K event and the threat to her precious computer.

I made tracks straight up the gut of Utah on Route 89 after burying Arizona in a toe hole of dirt near Kanab. I'd say the drive between Many Farms and Kayenta had been the most splendid of the trip. Perhaps as a joke the puzzle people had made Utah green which it was only in the highest elevation from junipers and other conifers. A cow had to work hard to fill its tummy. As a matter of fact I couldn't recall a single fat cow in Arizona. Maybe in both Arizona and Utah the cows just stand around getting skinny while they wait for the greening that comes after the summer monsoons. Meanwhile Utah thinks of itself as the beehive state, the California gull is the bird, plain old

"Industry" is the motto, and the sego lily, which I looked for in vain, is the state flower.

Marybelle called when I was driving around Panguitch looking in vain for a liquor store. For a change she was cheery rather than abrasive, complimenting me on raising such a fine son. I was wary waiting for her female hobnail boot to drop but it didn't happen other than for her to say that I must return to Vivian and nurse her back to health. She did complain about her lack of "sexual outlet" and I jokingly suggested she tour San Francisco's waterfront or hang out around one of the many local colleges. "Cliff, I'm searching for a worthy partner, a whole person, not a moron with a hard-on." I apologized with a trace of sincerity.

Utah would be a grand state if you could subtract Salt Lake City, the traffic of which wrung my soul into a dishrag. By the time I reached a rest stop north of the city I was actually trembling. I sat there at a picnic table vowing to never drive through a big city again. This would cost time and inconvenience but so what? When a blue-haired lady passes you an inch away going eighty while talking on a cell phone you fear for the Republic. Was it for this that the seagulls devoured the grasshoppers and saved the Mormon crops?

I reached Dillon, Montana, at nightfall feeling dumb as a post for having driven fifteen hours. I had three drinks and ate a mediocre slab of rare roast beef. I drove back to my humble motel and fell asleep in the parking lot quite happy to be cold. When I awoke at 2:00 a.m. there was a truly ugly little dog sitting outside my car door having smelled the piece of leftover roast beef I took from the restaurant in a doggy bag. I gave him the meat and despite my gift he growled when I patted his head. In my room I tried to turn the print of the sad-eyed donkey with a lei of flowers around its neck so I wouldn't have to look at it but it was stuck to the wall to prevent that. I fell asleep wishing Marybelle were perched on my nose like a gryphon.

MONTANA REDUX

I had the slowest morning start of my trip. I was still be-
numbed at daylight by the overlong drive but there was no
point in chiding myself further. I clicked on the Weather
Channel then fell back asleep after learning that Montana
would be in the mideighties which beat the shit out of the
over-hundred-degree weather I had been enduring to the
south along with everyone else who lived there. I awoke
again sinfully late at nine with last night's little dog growling and scratching at the door. I let him in and he made a
quick circle and then, determining I had nothing more for
him to eat, made a beeline back to the door. I decided at that
moment to adopt him if he was a genuine stray or had been
abandoned by someone staying at the motel. He somewhat
resembled the dog of my dreams running through the Alps
among the miniature elephants.

I had an irritating hard-on and reminded myself that I must stay high-minded for my project. I glanced in the mirror while rinsing my face with cold water to wake up. I whispered "Devouring time blunt thou the lion's paws," in honor of Shakespeare whom I still liked to read now and then for the same reason I listen to Mozart with pleasure fifty years after my mother introduced me to him. I tried to dismiss a pinprick of homesickness beneath my breastbone but then thought that homesickness like marital love was mostly a habit. What I missed was no longer there or on the verge of disappearing. I mean Lola was in dog heaven and the farm which had been sold to a stockbroker and his family from Chicago was to become a horse operation. The barn and my cozy workshop would likely be remodeled into stables, the orchard uprooted for pasture, and our old home razed in favor of what Viv said would be "French provincial" whatever that was. I consoled myself with the idea that there was freedom in having this large portion of your past vaporize. Fuimus fumus, or something like that, said Thomas Wolfe, my hero when I was a senior in high school. I think it meant that our life goes up in smoke.

At the motel desk a lady in curlers (blue) explained to me that the little dog who was named Bob belonged to one of the girls who cleaned rooms. She said that Bob was a pest but everyone seemed to like his obnoxious attitude. She also said that Bob liked beef but refused chicken and pork and any other kind of snack.

In the car I became distracted by the idea that as a displaced person I had no central location from which to do

some minimal research for my project. The bird names that
very much needed changing would only require east and
west bird books and my imagination which was not exactly
rampant. The states posed problems which could only be
solved by some library work. The *Encyclopedia Britannica* or
the simpler *World Book Encyclopedia* would suffice to jog my
imagination on the many states I hadn't visited. Perhaps I
had encountered a life's work too late in life? Marybelle was
a whiz on the computer and could easily get me needed information but I didn't want her horning in with advice. All
of those years as a nickel-plated farmer had made my brain
a shabby compass. I ruminated like the cattle I raised but
lacked their three stomachs to digest the information at hand.
Perhaps the dozen times I had read Ralph Waldo Emerson's
"Self-Reliance" had made me a unique individual but the
exact contents of my person had yet to be determined. I was
a bundle of intentions but was missing my mother's overused,
loathsome word "pluck," one of those Horatio Alger words
where if you have *pluck* you can pull yourself up by your
bootstraps and make your mark in the world.

What I really needed was breakfast having driven
away from Dillon without it. Last evening's beef hadn't
been aged enough and was rubbery though it was good
enough for little Bob the wonder dog. Bob's forthrightness
about his desires made me recall that my soundest thinking had taken place while I was fishing or trimming cherry
trees. There were no cherry trees hereabouts but lots of
rivers. Dad used to say we love rivers because that's what
we're made up of, that our blood vessels and veins and
arteries were rivers of sorts. I've never been confident of

the truth of this but it made a kind of sense. Mother said after Dad died that he had never been too good at reality but he kept his job.

I turned off in Melrose with the OnStar buzzing but I didn't answer it because I figured that my thoughts on my project demanded my complete attention and I had already been diverted by my hunger and the sight of a fishing tackle shop. As an English major I was familiar with the stories of dozens of writers trying to get their work done amid the multifarious diversions of the world and the hurdles of their own vices. A professor had said that what saved writers is that they, like politicians, had the illusion of destiny which allowed them to overcome obstacles no matter how nominal their work. Destiny seemed to be a religious concept on the order of the Methodist idea of predestination.

At a restaurant and bar called the Hitch'n Post a winsome, Spanish-looking girl served me eggs with biscuits and sausage gravy plus a sausage patty. A codger sitting next to me eyed my plate while eating a bowl of cornflakes.

"Lucky you. That's the Montana heart-stopper breakfast. Haven't had it since my quintuple bypass," he said.

I couldn't very well reply to this so I asked him how far away was the Big Hole River and he said about two hundred yards due west. My friend AD used to fish this river after he got out of medical school and told me to be sure to take a look at it. The beautiful waitress took my plate away without looking at me and I thought again that when you reach sixty younger women tend to put you in a biological Dumpster. She was transfixed by a young man in a wheelchair so I couldn't exactly say "lucky him."

I sat out in the car for a while pondering this mo-
mentous morning and my project began to take shape. I
certainly had no intention of becoming a writer. I'm too
much of a noun person to be a writer. They have to spend
a lot of time inflating the peripheries to fill out a book.
Their minds daily run to their work while I'm a simple
walker. All I wanted to do is change the names of specific
birds and states that had seemed to demand my attention
for a long time. But now, sitting in this car after ten in the
morning in mid-July I felt called to do so. I don't mean
like Moses and his burning bush or Paul on the way to
Damascus, just a retired farmer who sees a job that needs
to get done.

I drove past the tackle shop to take a look at the river
for its hopefully soothing effects. I parked the car and stood
in the middle of the bridge looking down into the mystery
of the water. I needed to consider certain pratfalls in my
calling. For instance, would I use too much alcohol for in-
spiration or for sedation if my mind becomes too rampantly
spirited? My Hart Crane alarm button went off. When I was
a college junior I waffled over the subject for a term paper
and my impatient professor assigned me Hart Crane. He had
rejected my idea for Edna St. Vincent Millay whom he referred to as "a bourgeois lust-crazed street slut." This was
in the sixties when "bourgeois" was a swear word and my
frizzy-haired assistant professor would wear his bell-bottoms
at a student café in the evening and say "All the power to the
people." I was never sure what people he meant.

Anyway, Hart Crane provided a truly miserable experience that spring. What an incredibly unhappy life I thought

wandering among the flowers along the Cedar River on Michigan State's lavishly landscaped campus. Hart Crane made me thankful for my own daffy, kind father. Crane's father was one of those nasty-minded Republican business-men that had been a curse on the body of our country. Crane was a hopeless drunk in his early twenties and committed suicide by jumping off a boat called the *Orizaba* in the Car-ibbean when he was thirty-two. Without liberal amounts of alcohol Crane couldn't compose his lovely but largely inscru-table poems which were so overwhelming compared to the torpor of Sandburg and Stephen Vincent Benét. I vowed right then staring down at the river not to use alcohol to fa-cilitate my project, or maybe just a little bit.

There was a specific anxiety in the tackle shop when I noted that the fly rods cost as much as seven hundred dol-lars. When I had entered the shop the owner was at his desk and computer and I thought I saw a naked lady on the screen but he quickly tapped an erase button. I browsed until I sweated, not wanting to spend a bunch of money when AD would bring out my equipment in a couple of weeks. The single rod I had brought along was a junky five-piece travel rod that I loathed.

"This stuff would set a man back an arm and a leg," I said.

"That's a forty-grand SUV you got out front."

"It's a loaner from my son."

"I got a cheap beginner's outfit."

"I've been trout fishing for fifty years."

"Then it doesn't matter what you use if you're any good."

He rummaged in a storage room in the back and came up with a somewhat delaminated outfit he had found in the river and reconditioned. I bought it for fifty bucks. I figured I didn't need waders because it was warm enough to wade in sneakers which proved not quite true. I drove down to an area called Notch Bottom, a name with a sexual tinge, and after an hour the water was so cold I couldn't feel my legs. I didn't care because I was catching and releasing brown trout plus seeing birds I'd never seen before. I fished about nine hours until twilight with the delight my little brother had when he would throw himself into the pond behind the barn.

MONTANA
REDUX II

When I stepped into the river near Notch Bottom I had
presumed it to be knee deep but the clarity of the water made
the depth an illusion and I plunged in to my breast. I sucked
in air mightily and felt my peter retreat into my body. Oh
well, I thought, tossing my two remaining now wet cigarettes
onto the bank where I might find them later all dried out
after my unpleasant baptism.

I fished and fished. At first there was no hatch so I
used a wet fly, an olive wooly bugger, but then after an
hour at about noon insects appeared that resembled the
green drakes back home and I caught a half-dozen brown
trout on a dry fly, a size-sixteen Adams which was invented
in Michigan. There was a hiatus in the action and I slept for
an hour on the bank. I wasn't sure how long because my
pocket watch had stopped with its dunking. When I awoke
I saw a mother moose and her calf disappearing into the

greenery of a cottonwood flat across the river. At mid-afternoon another insect arrived in plenitude and the river was covered with the circular dimples of rising fish. I successfully imitated the insect with size-fourteen caddis. I later found out the insect was a spruce moth. I was terribly thirsty but didn't dare drink the river water because of giardia, a parasite, but in the late afternoon I found a rivulet, a tiny spring emerging from the rock face of a cliff. I filled my sweaty hat and drank what seemed the best water of my life. In the early evening I caught a brown trout over three pounds on a deer hair coachman, a fish that would have been a life trophy up in Michigan. I confess tears formed when I slipped this divine creature back into its watery home.

I noticed the oncoming darkness and spent a full half hour thrashing my way through the bush back to my vehicle. I had found the two cigarettes and while smoking I renamed the western tanager the "firebird" in honor of Stravinsky whom I learned to love because my mother didn't. If Viv was around when Stravinsky was on NPR she'd yell "turn that shit off." Still with all of those memory nodules of unpleasant difficulties I felt a fondness for Viv. Early in our marriage when Robert was little the two of them would sometimes come trout fishing with me. Viv would bring a picnic basket featuring a fried chicken recipe passed down from her mother. You have to fry the chicken in home-made lard, not the store-bought kind. You soak the chicken overnight in buttermilk adding lots of Tabasco, then flour it and fry. Since I hadn't eaten since breakfast and it was nearly dark the idea of this fried chicken was maddening. When it was late May or early June Viv and Robert would pick lots of morel mushrooms and when we got home we'd have trout and fresh morels for supper.

Unfortunately by the time I reached the Hitch'n Post the kitchen was closed so a big meal was out of the question but the barmaid made me a very thick ham and swiss on rye plus nuked a bowl of beef barley soup. When I washed up, I looked comically awful in the toilet mirror: sunburned, tiny leaves and sticks in my hair and clothes, dirty hands and face, and sweaty clothes. I had wrestled all day with my first love. While I ate it came to me that I wasn't in first-rate mental shape when I had left Michigan, and perhaps for some time afterward. The fishing had opened a window in my mind's room and the new fresh air and light had made my state of mind on my departure grim indeed. Wife. Farm. Dog. Gone. What is left: Me, Viv, Robert.

A hand waved in front of my face. The tackle store owner had sat down beside me and I hadn't noticed it. We talked about fishing but after my second drink I was too wobbly and drowsy to continue. I walked the hundred yards to my motel, the Sportsman's Lodge, forgetting my vehicle and stumbling along in the dark, laughing as I figured out that my share of the farm, my life's work, came out to a profit of four grand a year, not much in today's terms.

I was physically exhausted and my legs were still cold from the river and I slept the sleep of Cora, a family idiom. Cora was an old sow that gave us half a dozen litters in successive years and then came up dry. As a child I wept so piteously when Dad was going to butcher her that he relented and said that she was now my responsibility. She was old, very obese, and mostly slept, weighing probably five hundred.

I was getting a little too big but Cora would let my little
brother Teddy ride on her back though she'd only take a
few steps before falling back to sleep. Dad said that Cora
would die from sleep, fat, and no exercise so all by myself,
I think I was eleven at the time, I rigged a circular narrow
passageway out of a hundred yards of fencing and fed Cora
at the furthest part of the circle from the pigpen which abut-
ted the corncrib. We grew a lot of fruit: apples, sweet and
sour cherries, Concord grapes for Dad's awful wine, pears,
and peaches. Cora dearly loved fruit and when I'd dump a
couple of gallons of it in her trough she'd close her eyes and
gobble with pleasure. With ordinary hog slop and corn she'd
keep her eyes open. After her dinner she'd stop for a couple
of naps on her way back home to her shelter under the corncrib. Often she'd quiver and churn her feet while asleep as
if she was dreaming and Dad said she was likely dreaming
about food. When she finally died, in her sleep of course, it
took me three days to dig a hole big enough to bury her. My
little brother Teddy tried to jump in the hole with Cora but
Dad held him tight during the grave service which Mom
didn't attend. Afterward Teddy would put his ear to the
ground at the grave site.

I felt good in the morning what with a nice dream about
Viv's Stroganoff, her other good dish besides fried chicken.
She'd use a pint of fine Jersey cow cream got from a neighbor and also reconstituted dried morels. I drank my coffee
holding on to this dream state and decided to call her before breakfast. To cut the cream I'd eat some wild leeks I
would dig up and pickle. We'd use our own best beef.

I can't say the conversation made me warm all over. It

was mostly Viv spinning figures in real estate language to the effect that "tax wise" I'd have to be her employee while I remodeled the bungalow and that it could be amortized if I'd let her sell the back twenty of the forty acres. I said no because this was the location of the hillock where I'd sit with the Indian who couldn't talk because of his war wound. I'd have a life lease and she would retain title. I asked, "What if you die first" and she said, "Then it would go to Robert, stupid." Not very charming. I also asked if I'd get paid and she answered "a little something," adding that under no condition could I bring my "wicked waitress" onto the property. I teased her with the question of whether she expected us to remarry and she said, "No, I want to keep my options open. I'm just lonely for you now and then." That was that. There's always been something icky to me about the word "compromise," perhaps because of all of my reading in the New England transcendentalists, especially Emerson and Thoreau, and also the English Romantics. Did Byron compromise? Not hardly, but then the long road from Lord Byron to this English major fan didn't exist. My senses hadn't totally left me. I had lost the farm and Lola and the thread between me and Viv was fragile indeed. I had lost much of my past but not all of it. I could live out my life at Grandpa's place nearly enveloped by state forest. The tiny gravel road leading to it passed through a dense cedar swamp, and then came the scrubby clearing and the old Sears bungalow built in the twenties, and the other tar-paper shack. There was some reasonably good trout fishing and when I needed to look at a woman I could drive over to Cross Village on Lake Michigan or east to Pellston. I'd buy some good camping equipment and drive to the southwest in the winters, live in the desert, and Bert could be my teacher in this new area. I certainly wouldn't camp in his snake-infested yard. This would have to be enough.

The vision of the body of Bert's meth-ditzy girlfriend made me long for Marybelle so I made the mild mistake of calling her cell.

"Cliff, Cliff, Cliff, my heart cries for you as the song used to go. And other parts too. My life is blooming. Last evening I got the part of Blanche in the upcoming *A Streetcar Named Desire*. I don't get their choice of Stanley. He's a gay guy with thin arms. My life is blooming, Cliff, and it's all because you delivered me to your wonderful son. I just didn't belong in Morris, Minnesota. I'm a bright lights, big city girl. For instance this morning I absolutely knew my son had been captured by guerrillas in Africa."

"Gorillas or guerrillas?" I felt I had to say something.

"That's a good question. Did you know gorillas have miniature penises? About the size of a filter cigarette?"

"No I didn't know that."

"Anyway, I had coffee and said to myself, Marybelle, you don't really have a son so how can he be in Africa? In short, Cliff, I'm becoming less delusional in San Francisco."

And so on. My sexual needs seemed to diminish with the phone call and there was a vague pang of feeling sorry for myself. Dad once warned me about this when I was mourning the loss of a girlfriend to a quarterback. I was a lonely lineman. I moped and moped, and then when we were cutting wood on an icy October morning he told me that self-pity was a ruinous emotion. "Look at the world, not up your ass," he said. It took me a while to figure this out.

I went fishing and got caught in a violent hailstorm. It came from the west but I couldn't see far in that direction because of the mountains. I lost a very large brown trout that would have been the biggest of my life just before the fishing went dead. This trout had run downriver full blast through a narrow stretch that was too deep to wade and I had tried to crawl along the thick brush at the river's edge and then the line went slack. I had seen the thickened body of the fish right after he or she struck and was deciding an escape route.

Anyway, the hailstorm struck when I was sitting on a log musing on the trout and what I thought might be sonic booms from jet fighters in the west. All experienced anglers know that the odds of landing a big brown trout are small indeed. I was inattentive to the change in the weather because it occurred to me that it was likely dishonest to change the name of a bird or state if I hadn't actually seen the bird or visited the state. I certainly had no firsthand experience of artistic integrity but now the theoretical aspects loomed large. Some sort of thrush I didn't recognize was staring at me from a nearby bush. I had heard that during migration thrushes will stop for a nine-second nap. You heard it right, nine seconds. It was then that the hail hit from a black sky that had crept up on me. I fled across the river, stumbling in the current because I was trying to shield my eyes from the stinging ice pellets. I fell face forward and drifted in the current for a way trying to catch my breath. It was eerie what with the river covered with a moving sheet of white-ness. I crawled up a steep muddy bank and headed upstream to where I had seen a very old abandoned Dodge Power Wagon loaded with rocks out of which grew grass and wild-flowers. In fact with my head down I walked smack into the truck then scraped my back crawling under it. Holy shit, my ass was freezing. The temperature must have dropped from the high seventies to the forties. I hadn't eaten break-fast, instead ordering a roast beef sandwich to go, but the bread was soaked with river water. Who can eat bread soaked in river water? I chewed hungrily on the meat and onions looking up at the greasy undercarriage of the truck. It was then that I thought I might take some sort of artistic vows for my project. The *non serviam* of James Joyce wouldn't work because I had already spent so much of my life serving cattle, the cherry orchard, not to speak of Vivian after she took on a real estate job and gave up on our home.

MONTANA
REDUX III

Dawn and on my way east toward Reed Point I began to think of my plans as a little ill formed. I didn't remember seeing a motel in the tiny village much less the library that I'd need for the project. I pulled off the interstate near Whitehall and looked at the map determining that Livingston might be the best destination, remembering that when I passed through Big Timber it seemed rather small.

The morning had begun with a lurch. The NPR news from Iraq made me heartsick and I turned to a classical station only to hear that Borodin music that had been used for *Kismet*. This was the singular piece of classical music that Viv loved, and I loathed it. I'd hear her from the shower, especially if she had been into the schnapps, singing. "Take my hand, I'm a stranger in Paradise." I certainly knew I wasn't the object of her fantasies. She intermixed her reading of conspiracy novels with romantic novels. I had looked at a couple and noted that when hero and heroine fucked they tended to fall back on great waves of nothingness. At one point I had hidden her *Kismet* album in the pump shed and she had, guessing me as the guilty party, defiantly bought three more copies in Traverse City. What's more, she had taken to singing the song when she wanted to irritate me.

I limited myself to a few minutes of pondering marriage. Marybelle had said that she loved to act because you got to be "many people, not just one." Of course she already was. Maybe one of the problems with Viv and me is that each of us was just one person. Perhaps this came about because when you are born and raised in the country neuroses are only minimally tolerated. You can be goofy if you're a good worker. In the upper Midwest stern duty always calls and to be late for work or a layabout is a crime against the state. You have your coffee and then feed your farm animals before you feed yourself. Trying to figure out the place of marriage's arduous dreariness became inscrutable parked there on the roadside. A raven watched me from a fence post and then turned around and pooped. I took this as a coincidence rather than a sign. In marriage ceremonies the word "twain" was used for that old-timey sacral feeling, also "asunder."

The OnStar buzzed and there was the thought of disabling it with a pistol. It was Robert and he sounded drunk and tearful.

"Dad, I've been up all night in a state of joy because my parents are getting back together."

"Well, I've turned toward home but we haven't exactly made a deal yet." It was 6:00 a.m. in San Francisco and I was expecting a mud bath.

"I worked out the GPS coordinates and you'll be living forty miles from each other which is not EXACTLY romantic but it's a start. I've had a lot of turmoil in my LIFE and those memories of you and Mom and me walking through the orchard at SUNSET holding hands has kept me going. I'm so grateful for the way you raised me. Thank you. Thank you."

"You're welcome." His voice was breaking and I began to sweat despite the coolish morning.

"Dad, the car is now in your name so you can terminate the phone service but please don't. It's a lifeline of our family."

He was sounding drowsy and we said our good-byes after a lame discussion of how I might help Viv with her diabetic diet which involved constant donut prevention. Put out the raging donut fires!

For the time being there would be no more puzzle pieces to toss away in the watercourse, not anyway until I made my next voyage which I assumed would be in the coming winter. When you don't have much to do, why rush? I'd have to go home through the same states where likely no one has found those small waterlogged pieces. My dream had forbade recrossing the Mississippi so I would have to cut way north up by International Falls, a vehicular end run so as not to defile my dreamscape. Many artists have received oracular hot tips from their sleeping brains. I certainly wasn't an artist yet but I had a sense of calling not unlike James Joyce near the estuary when he saw the girl pull her dress up her thighs. Art loves biology.

My thoughts drifted back to a nasty incident in the Hitch'n Post bar the night before. I was having a bountiful nightcap after eating a famous Montana dish, the chicken-fried steak with cream gravy, and idly talking to a nicely dressed woman in her thirties who was a grade school teacher south of Melrose in Dillon. She was what we used to think of as a "plain Jane" but in her case so plain that she was quite attractive. She also wore an ever-so-slight lilac scent, an odor that always gets my hormones churning. We were talking about the pleasures and horrors of teaching when two men dressed as cowboys entered, one very big and one small, both a little drunk. She waved and said, "There's my husband," which surprised me because she had said they'd only moved from Seattle the year before and I hadn't expected she'd married a cowboy in Seattle. However, I was gradually figuring out that the real cowboys wore hats with sweat-stained brims, had severely weather-beaten skin, and their clothes tended to be frayed. Anyway, the smaller one lurched between us half knocking his wife off her stool at the bar. He was wearing newish western clothes and an absurd turquoise bolo tie.

"Watch it buddy," he said as if I was the one who shoved his wife.

"Of course," I said shrugging.

"I might just kick your ass," he fairly shrieked.

"Cut that shit out, Freddy," his large friend said, rolling his eyes to apologize to me.

"I think I better kick your ass," Freddy said grabbing my shirt.

"That seems unlikely. You're a smallish cowpoke and I'm a large farmer." I was smiling to try to defuse the situation.

"Freddy, you turd!" his plain-Jane wife hissed. She grabbed his ear, twisting it, and then led him out of the bar with his head leaning into her hand. That was that. An old lady and a couple of actual cowboys laughed loudly.

I was diverted by NPR when a disembodied male voice said that a mere teaspoon of a neutron star would weigh a billion tons. As a literature person I at first missed the point and wondered at the preposterous strength of the teaspoon. I was amazed at my own density while closing in on the fair-sized city of Bozeman. I had mulled it over and decided that I didn't need a close-by library, only a simple book that characterized our fifty states, plus my bird books. I would begin by changing the names of the states and birds I already knew and then with travel and bird-watching gradually complete the project. I was saddened by the idea that I might not finish the work before I died, a natural enough fear. Keats wrote, "When I have fears that I may cease to be before my pen has glean'd my teeming brain . . ." That was throwing the raw meat on the floor in a lovely way. My brain wasn't exactly teeming but nature is heraldic and birds simply don't deserve the banal names we've given them.

While filling up at a service station outside of Bozeman I was impressed once again by the fact that there is no tourniquet for a self-harried brain. The young man at

the cash register had tiny rings in his eyebrows, nose, and
ears, perhaps a sign of the new West. It turned out he was
from Columbus near Reed Point where I shouldn't stay if I
wanted any "action." When I said I preferred solitude he
said that I'd have solitude coming out my ass in Reed Point
and that Livingston was "chock-full of willing pussy." Back
in my car I questioned why I wanted solitude when I had
just had a twenty-five-year dose of it while working the farm.
And I was headed for a lot more of it while I remodeled
Grandpa's house where it would be a dozen-mile drive to
even look at a female. It was also doubtful if the visiting AD
would tolerate Reed Point. At deer camp AD would drive
to Grand Marais or Newberry and close the bars at night.
He reminded me of a poet who was one of my roommates
at a squalid little bungalow on Lake Lansing when I was a
junior in college. Every night he'd go out carousing quoting a line of Rilke saying, "Only in the rat race of the arena
can the heart learn to beat." I presumed this man Rilke to
be a pretty racy poet but when I looked at one of his books
I found out otherwise.

I stopped at the Country Bookshelf in Bozeman and
bought a compendium of the fifty states designed for young
adults, also two books on local grizzly bears and rattlesnakes. If I climbed a wilderness mountain I wanted to take
precautions with the local fauna. The bookstore had a number of attractive clerks who didn't make eye contact with
me but looked just above my hairline reminding me again
of my safe place in the biological Dumpster.

In Livingston it didn't take long to find a good place to
stay through the chamber of commerce because there had

been a cancellation on a temporary rental on Ninth Street Island in the Yellowstone River. On the way out to look at the place I called AD on his cellular because the rental price was expensive. AD said he had a pretty woman in the stirrups in the other room so that in order to be professional he was thinking about "mom and apple pie." He would be out in five days and wanted reassurance that our quarters were near the "night life" whatever that turned out to be. He also said that he had hurt an ankle on a hike and that I should hire a drift boat and guide for the week.

The house was fine and I ponied up the dough to the rental agent, a lumpy woman who was still slightly attractive, as were nearly all women the further away I got from Marybelle. I wandered around the island after examining the suitable kitchen utterly relieved that I'd be able to cook for myself. The main channel of the Yellowstone was west of the house and looked so large as to be spooky for wading but there was a wide and shallower fishable channel to the east and I felt simply enthralled to have fishing near my doorstep. Since it was hot and clear I decided to take a snooze, go grocery shopping, and fish later in the afternoon.

I lay back in a La-Z-Boy chair and in sleep was drawn vividly to Viv (excuse the pun) in a dream so lurid I woke in a half hour in a sweat. The year after we were married and well before she was pregnant with Robert, Viv and I had met for the weekend with a dozen college friends at Houghton Lake, a mildly squalid resort area favored by the blue-collar crowd of Flint and Detroit. We all met at the Lagoona Beach Motel and when we checked in I questioned the smartass desk clerk whether the correct spelling shouldn't be "Laguna" and he said, "What are you, a English major?" and everyone laughed. Viv and I were antidrug but we ended up smoking a lot of pot and drinking too much that weekend. Marijuana turned Viv into an implacable sexual tigress and I returned home with actual bruises. She did a lot of hooting and hollering to be frank. We all went nude swimming at night and I was so stoned that when I was underwater I couldn't find the surface. Now thirty-seven years later I woke up pissed off because I was sure I saw a guy named Bob playing with Viv's big tits.

MONTANA
REDUX IV

I came fully awake in my chair in a condition of panic because when emerging from the edge of sleep I realized this August date was the first anniversary of our fatal high school reunion, a day that will live in infamy or something like that. We had been lukewarm about attending in the first place, especially me, because I hadn't wanted to drive back from Mullett Lake on a Sunday evening what with all of those pissed-off tourists heading to urban prisons. And little did I know I would be driving back to the farm with a boozed-up Viv with shameless grass stains on her knees.

Enough! Enough, my heart yelled at itself as I struggled out of the reclining chair, the knob to bring it upright being stuck. There was the question in college of whether or not Thoreau had ever had the pleasure of sexual union or did he remain a monk of nature? The school reunion had blasted my life apart with the power of a Shiite car bomb and my

errant thoughts told me there were pieces that still needed
to be rejoined.

Luckily it was late enough in the afternoon that my
mind drifted to creaturely hunger and the idea of a sizable
pork steak in an iron skillet displaced the battering of divorce. Viv never liked pork steak thinking of it as "poor
people's food" so Lola and I would share it for lunch. A
history professor had said that pork had fueled our west-
ward course of empire. Pigs happily followed the wagon
trains that carried their evening meal while cattle would
wander off.

On the way to downtown Livingston to do my shopping I stopped at a bar called the Owl (a proper name for a
bird, especially barn owl) for a pick-me-up and to find out
a place to buy non-factory-farm pork. It was a bar populated by locals rather than tourists and they all seemed to
drink pretty fast. Working folks are rarely sippers. Back in
high school we'd have chug-a-lug contests and my friend
Bert learned to pour down a bottle of beer without swallowing and won all the contests though there were no prizes
except to be drunk.

At the Owl I got my pork instructions and also met an
acerbic man in his forties who gave me his fishing guide card.
On the way out I remembered that AD had said he'd ordered two cases from a wine store and that I should pick
them up. I never go into such places finding them as intimidating as men's clothing stores. I'd buy a half gallon of Gallo
Hearty Burgundy at the grocery store, though I admit when
I went to AD's house I enjoyed his penchant for expansive
French wine but then he said he made his wine budget by

indulging a few hypochondriacs. The two cases cost $470 so I was pleased that AD had paid ahead by credit card. It seemed a lot of wine for the five days that AD would be there but then he tended to drag home "lassies" after the bar closed.

While I was loading the wine into the Tahoe I turned in order to listen to two attractive young women leaning against an older Volvo parked next to me. Women who have inferred that I'm not very interesting admit that I'm a good listener and this includes eavesdropping. One of the women was pushing a baby stroller containing a fat little rascal who was watching me with blank suspicion. She was explaining to the other who was obviously a ditz like Marybelle that her baby had only learned to crawl backward which meant that the objects of his desire were always receding. I found this startling and full of meaning. The other woman prattled on about her upcoming divorce and used words like "iconic" and "embedded" and "closure." She had found her husband's obsession with fishing "too phallocentric" for words. Once when we had visited Viv's cousin down in Suttons Bay I had heard a group of women using such language but I had no idea where it came from. Even commonsensical Viv used to have only "problems" but now had "issues."

On the way back to the rental I tuned in the livestock report and laughed at the idea that I would have made real money on my cattle this year mostly because Canadian beef was still embargoed over mad cow disease. It reminded me of the year the cherry crop in southern Michigan (a state that perhaps should be called Ojibway?) froze out in the budding stage and our crop up north made substantial money for a change. In farming your good luck often depends on someone else's bad. Toyota is ascendant while Ford mopes, that sort of thing.

What pleasure I had cooking my own dinner and there on the desk in the corner were my tablets, pens, and books, ready for my life's work to commence. I dipped my massive pork steak in beaten egg to which I had added Tabasco, salt, and pepper, then rolled it in Italian bread crumbs. I used twelve-dollar olive oil which made me shudder at the point of purchase. I added three cloves of finely chopped garlic and a tin of anchovies to my salad. Life on the road doesn't present strong flavors except nasty ones, the deliquescent gravy that arrives in barrels. I certainly had experienced none of the bandied-about food revolution which was obviously limited to cities and folks with fat wallets.

I was silly and imprudent and drank a whole bottle of AD's wine that he especially liked called Sang des Cailloux Vacqueyras which he explained to me meant "blood of the stones." AD has been to France many times but the young woman who teaches languages at the high school said that she had overheard AD at a party and the French he spoke was hokum nonsense like that on the restaurant skits on *A Prairie Home Companion.* I asked AD about this and he only said that the sound is more meaningful than the words "just like dogs barking." To be sure, AD is a puzzle.

What with a full bottle of wine in my system I fished poorly after dinner and after tangling my leader and snapping off flies several times I settled on sitting on a boulder and watching night fall so slowly that it seemed to be rising up out of the river. I stumbled back to the house in the pitch dark, put on a pot of coffee intending to work, then fell asleep in a chair waking at 2:00 a.m. to the sound of bullbats through the screen door flying after insects. It was an electric moment and I heard myself talking aloud, "I have no more time for self-doubt which is a profession in itself for English majors. I must follow my star even if it turns out to be one of those squiggly motes floating through my eyeball." I thought how preposterous it was that anyone would try to paste a decal of sanity on our time. Like Thoreau I must walk to the beat of my own drummer. Ten years of teaching and twenty-five of farming had beaten my youthful idealism senseless but now I felt that it had begun to burble up again in me. In late April I'd take a pitchfork and rake out to the woodlot with Lola leading the way and free up the spring of its detritus of mud, leaves, and sticks. It was quite beautiful to see the pure water pour upward, flooding the surrounding wild leeks, skunk cabbage, snake grass, and trillium. I had abandoned my purest impulses for a lifetime of toil and now they were arising again.

Sitting there at the desk in the middle of the night with a mug full of coffee I could barely see the newish moon through the opaque window which showed my reflection with the moon perched on my hairline. Obviously my road trip had begun to tug my mind back from the so-called real world to the world of books I had so valued in my late teens and early twenties. I had always thought of my university experience as largely unpleasant which in truth it was, but now the ghosts of all those books and ideas were returning. Doubtless the sexual depth charge of Marybelle had loosened me up for which I felt oddly grateful. Right after college I had dreamed of having what I thought of as a Henry Miller experience and it had lain in wait until I was sixty, perhaps too late in life to want the experience repeated right away. Holy cow! What a woman.

Now in the night with my empty tablet before me I felt like it was early spring calving time and I was sitting out in the shed with a thermos checking and rechecking my mother cows for any birth difficulties. They were so patient in their discomfort and when one in labor leaned against me for solace I felt of some use in this world.

It wasn't until 4:00 a.m. after several cups of coffee and a glass of bourbon to calm my nerves that a small lightning bolt struck. I had been pacing the room, glancing now and then at a bookshelf full of the sort of riffraff books bought and abandoned by people on vacation, you know, *How to Make a Fortune by Cheating*, or *The Zen of Chocolate*. In the corner I discovered *Atlas of the North American Indian*, a Livingston Library book three years overdue. My moment of "Eureka!" came instantly. Each of our United States must have an Indian name for a tribe that originally inhabited the area. Simple as that. My skin fairly tingled and I poured myself an ample 4:00 a.m. nightcap to celebrate the moment. I walked out into the yard and looked up at the stars remembering Lorca's line about "the enormous night straining its waist against the Milky Way." To the south I could see the outlines of the Absaroka Mountains, the largest of which I intended to climb before AD arrived in a few days. If not God I would be closer to these resplendent stars that seemed to be boring tiny holes in my head, a trepanation to ease the pressure of my own creation.

I went to bed but my mind was whirling and then
cranking like a Bach organ fugue. When I closed my eyes
I would see mountains and stars, but also Cora my pet sow,
Marybelle's pussy descending toward my face, Lola carrying around a dead muskrat in her mouth as if it were a
trophy, Viv screeching at me because I hadn't learned a
particular polka step, and then real horrors from the classroom long ago like trying to teach my bored nitwits how
to diagram sentences and discuss participles or current
events. They were assigned to watch Walter Cronkite
every evening but rarely did so. And worse yet my one
brief college roommate, the poet, who would eat Franco-
American spaghetti right out of the can and keep saying
"The arts are a cruel mistress."

Obviously I hadn't needed to drink an entire pot of
coffee to create whatever, a neophyte's mistake. At first
light I went outside, sat in a lawn chair and listened for
birds but there weren't many with August being the molting season. If your feathers are changing and you can't fly
well, just shut up. Mosquitoes were biting me but I didn't
care because I was dwelling on the question of whether
Michigan should be renamed after the Ottawa, Chippewa,
or Potawatomi. The last would be a little awkward on the
tongue to be widely accepted.

MONTANA REDUX V

It was odd indeed to finally fall asleep at a time that I had been getting up as a farmer for twenty-five years. Through half-closed eyes I had watched the nuthatch storing seeds in the bark of a large willow and decided to call it "banker bird" as I have read that nuthatches will store as many as 300,000 seeds a season, dozens of times what they'll ever need. Before I stumbled inside to bed to escape the mosquitoes I stared long and hard at the mountain I intended to climb when I woke up which would not be at dawn because it was already dawn. I was prepared to fail at mountain climbing because I knew vaguely there was more to it than wandering up a steep ascent. My dissipating thoughts of life in terms of victory or defeat came along willy-nilly from a culture that pretended that life was far more solid than it actually was. The edges were actually blurred and moved along with the infinitely variable shape of a river.

I got up at nine and ate a fried-egg-and-pork-steak sandwich. You don't climb a mountain with a bowl of Cheerios for fuel, or so I suspected. I had a rare headache from my middle of the night pot of coffee and no aspirin at hand because as a man of moderate nonartistic habits I never had headaches. The pain transferred itself to a heartache when I crossed the Ninth Street Bridge and saw a girl jogging with a geezer like myself, likely her father or a man with secret powers which would mean vast wealth. The girl wore rose-colored shorts and her butt and legs were beyond world-class, so fine that my heart turned itself up a notch. I slowed down in order that my neurons might duly record this butt's splendor and when I passed I noted that her cool, intense face signified a true "Belle Dame Sans Merci." I had quickly become horny as a toad and called Marybelle on OnStar, receiving the message that her "boss" wouldn't allow personal calls except at lunch or after six. Despite wanting to hear her sexy voice this amused me. When Robert was in the eighth grade he directed the seniors in a play mustering the authority of a drill sergeant. I stopped in the Livingston park and pretended to be looking for something in the front seat to allow the joggers to pass. The girl gave me a scornful smile as if knowing what I was up to. Her companion was soaked with sweat and wheezing while she was dry. AD told me that he treats several older joggers who have lost inches in height from compacting hip and knee joints. He also said that no creature in nature jogs.

My mountain climb was a tad farcical. I definitely rediscovered my age. Though I had always been a habitual walker my weeks in the car had delaminated my legs. I had

called the chamber of commerce at breakfast for information on the trailhead and when I parked at Pine Creek I
forgot my canteen of water because I was reading a sign
that advised being "careful" about grizzly bears. Since they
have the decided advantage I wondered how one went
about being careful? I certainly wasn't driving all the way
back to town for an aerosol can of the recommended pepper spray.

I walked upward for four hours taking exactly fifty-
three brief breaks, holding on to trees for support. My legs
jiggled, wobbled, and twitched of their own accord. My feet
ached in their ankle-high basketball shoes. I had a brief view
of the end of the tree line when I turned around at 4:00 p.m.
at which point two elderly ladies (about my age) whizzed
by me smiling in their hiking outfits. It was painful to my
shins to walk down and when I met two young men coming toward me who saw my grimace one quipped, "Buy a
pair of hiking boots." No shit. I stopped and stood under a
small waterfall after laying my billfold aside. I forgot my
billfold and had to return a ghastly hundred yards uphill to
fetch it at which point it occurred to me that one of the young
men reminded me of one of the three English-major classmates of mine at Michigan State who ended up committing
suicide within a few years of graduation. I wasn't the only
one who took life and literature seriously.

When I reached the Tahoe it was hot in the parking
lot and I nearly gagged on the warm water of my canteen.
My feet could barely work the gas and brake pedals. This
was clearly the nadir of my trip though I didn't realize on

the way to town the worst was yet to come as I had so
screwed up my leg muscles and tendons that I could barely
fish for three days. I was famished and I drove directly to
the Bistro which was across the street from the Owl Bar,
first stopping at the bar for two quick vodkas on ice. I ran
into the fishing guide who told me I looked like shit. I re-
plied that I had tried to climb a mountain and he said,
"Why?" before turning his attention back to the barmaid.

I sat at an outside table at the Bistro so I could smoke.
Lo and behold my waitress was the beauteous-butted jog-
ger who had worn the rose-colored shorts. It was early in
the dinner hour and she wasn't busy so we chatted. At first
she seemed inexplicably daffy. For instance when I asked
her about the health of her senior jogging partner she said
he was "just another capitalist chiseler" who had recently
moved to Montana, a Connecticut stockbroker who decided
he would become a painter. She was the daughter of a miner
from Butte, a union man, thus her old-style antirich lingo
that I hadn't heard much of since my dad died. She was a
student at the University of Montana in Missoula but in
October she was headed to Guatemala to work in a Catholic mission for orphans. My heart leapt when she said she
preferred older men like her dad but then she added that
she disapproved of drugs, alcohol, and sex. I ate a skirt steak
and the best French fries of my life and a big glass of red
wine while she dealt with three young business types two
tables away. When one of them grabbed her arm she said,
"Hands off cocksucker" and he blushed. They finished their
drinks and left and when she came back to my table she

asked why I looked crippled when I had crossed the street
from the Owl. I explained my mountain climbing misadven-
ture and she said, "Good for you for trying," adding that she
had a friend that did massage therapy if my muscles got
desperate. I couldn't help but ask her why she was anti sex,
drugs, and alcohol and she said it was partly religious but
mostly because everyone she knew had screwed up their
lives with sex, drugs, and alcohol. When I paid my bill and
left a big tip she laughed and said, "Even you old guys get
fucked up." I looked over and her Connecticut stockbroker
was glaring at us from the restaurant door. She whispered
to me that he paid her three hundred bucks to pose nude
and "he can't paint shit."

On the short drive home I resolved not to go back to
the Bistro and torture myself looking at and talking to the
waitress, whose name was Sylvia. I needed to become a
monk of my art and sketch out the new names of the states
before AD arrived in three days. At the rental I hobbled
down to the river and felt a flash of rage that the rich bas-
tard got to see Sylvia naked. I could barely draw a stick-
figure human but it wouldn't hurt for me to buy a sketch
pad and give it a try. For three hundred bucks I could buy
myself a permanent memory that might somehow help my
project. AD had quoted Freud saying that sexual repression
helped artists and writers create. Three hundred bucks was
a lot of money but was it if it facilitated my art? I was looking at long days remodeling Grandpa's house and it would
be nice to have a beautiful memory. The theme in literature
was called "carpe diem" which means "seize the day." Another Latin phrase I could recall from my student days was

"noli me tangere," or "don't touch me" which was the invisible sign on Sylvia's pussy.

I waddled back inside the house, grabbed the portable phone, and settled back in my La-Z-Boy chair. I called Sylvia and arranged to have a massage from her friend and also a posing session for the next morning. I asked her to bring along a sketch pad as I had left mine in San Francisco. "Have you ever owned a sketch pad?" she asked with bell-clear laughter, then hung up after I gave directions. I was a crippled old goat sitting there remembering a line of Shelley's that I loathed, "I fall upon the thorns of life! I bleed!"

I slept in the La-Z-Boy from eight until two in the morning. I eased out of the chair with difficulty and crawled around the floor for a few minutes to relax my muscles enough so I could stand. Fuck mountains, I thought. This time I made two cups of coffee rather than a full pot. I laid out my ball points and my intimidating empty tablet. Unlike teaching and farming where the future was full day by day I felt a specific and wonderful freedom as I made a draft of alternatives for many of the state names. There was a problem that the Indians were there before the states and consequently slipped over the borders that were later established. I had to make critical choices in the end but right now it was important to keep it open-ended. I had a glass of whiskey after an hour and exulted in the freedom of my mind at play. Thoreau had pointed out that a farm owned the farmer rather than vice versa but now I had gradually realized that I owned myself and could give myself to the highest calling, albeit late in life. I cautioned myself against the manic aspects of alcohol that might blur the fine lines of both art and life knowing full well that I wouldn't have had the craw to call Sylvia if I hadn't had the two vodkas at the Owl and the glass of wine with dinner. I recalled that a prominent Michigan writer of Irish decent had said that alcohol was the writer's black lung disease. I had been cagey with Sylvia, first ordering up the massage so she wouldn't be spooked visiting me alone. I had never received a massage before and was a bit uncertain if it would be money well spent or a stepping-stone.

I slept angelically from 4:00 a.m. until nine, had a light breakfast, showered, then sat down to wait, reading an article "Ten Easy Ways to Start a Conversation" in an old *Reader's Digest*. They didn't arrive at ten as promised. They didn't arrive at 10:30 or 11:00. Finally at 11:30 the masseuse, Brandy by name, showed up with a collapsible, portable gurney and set up administering pain. She said Sylvia was running late because her mother who was a "perfect bitch" had showed up from Butte. Brandy had nice features but was Germanically masculine and large. The massage was overwhelmingly unpleasant but after an hour I felt much less like a piece of physical detritus. I was, however, a mud puddle of despair over not seeing Sylvia naked. Brandy teased me while we were having iced tea out in the yard saying that she had read in the *New York Times* that male monkeys will give up lunch in order to see photos of female monkey butts. This was discouraging information about sexual slavery but then AD had already given me this bad news.

Finally at noon Sylvia came running up the driveway in her rose-colored shorts. She handed me a tiny sketchbook the size of a deck of cards saying, "I thought you should start your art career small. We'll have to reschedule." I was stricken and she gave me a gentle hug. Her eyes were slightly puffy from crying. Off they went.

MONTANA
REDUX VI

I stuck to home. The world was a dangerous place. I bore down on my art as if I were digging fence posts.

It was Friday morning before I could fish more than an hour and I would pick AD up at the Bozeman airport in the evening. In the forty-eight hours since I had seen Sylvia not five minutes had passed without my thinking of those rose-colored shorts but I had somehow managed to trans-figure her into a modern Beatrice, an unapproachable young woman who had fueled Dante's *Divina Commedia* as surely as pork had fueled our western movement to the mighty shores of the Pacific.

I was fishing in the side channel near the house but wading cautiously as my old legs had not quite recovered full mobility. I felt a modest glow because the fifty states were falling into shape and I had made a fine chicken soup for AD using a whole barnyard chicken I had bought at a health food store, a full head of garlic, fresh corn, sage leaves, and two tomatoes that were vaguely suspect. Montana is definitely not a garden state except for those with private gardens. AD talks a good game in terms of international cuisine but is too impatient to cook well. In separate years at deer camp when it was his turn to cook he served us rare pork roast and chicken bloody at the joint and no one was happy after a cold day in the woods.

I caught a small rainbow about a foot long and was on the verge of slipping it back into the water when I heard a voice from the willow thicket behind me. It was Sylvia.

"Don't let it go. I like to eat fish." She was actually breathing hard and sweating but then the temperature was at least ninety.

"Do you ever stop running?"

"I started running when I was twelve to get over my mom. I'm twenty-one now and still running and Mom is still Mom."

"What's wrong with her?" I walked toward her with the fish feeling the not very curious urge to lick the sweat off her body.

"Gambling. Poker machines in bars. Slot machines. Lottery tickets. Bus trips to Las Vegas. We lost our junky home in Butte. Dad kicked her out and now he lives in an apartment with my brother. I came over to see if you want me to pose?"

"I'm not so sure it's a good idea. I mean I feel embarrassed about the whole thing." Now I was standing in front

of her with my blood rushing into my face as if I were twelve
years old and had been caught jerking off in the Lutheran
church.

"I could use the money. That's why I was crying on
Wednesday. Mom stole six hundred bucks I hadn't put in
the bank."

"Okay," I said, with my brain becoming lime Jell-O
with chopped bananas. On the walk to the house I was
tongue-tied and answered questions with difficulty when she
wondered what I did for a living. When I said I was a retired farmer she was delighted because her grandfather on
her mother's side was a farmer from Big Sandy, Montana.
I also admitted to teaching school for ten years which
brought on a yawn. As we neared the house and zero hour
I became simultaneously giddy and goofy. I was on the verge
of buying a permanent memory and I didn't want terrorists
to attack before she took off her clothes. The purity of my
lust, however, was a tiny bit tempered by worrying about
her mother's bad behavior. Nasty relatives are always entering our deepest male fantasies.

"In the green morning/the cult of love is possible," I
said, quoting a poem, as she opened the door and bowed me
into the house.

"Not with me buster," she said glancing around. "I
don't see your easel! You'll have to settle for sketching." She
tossed me the little sketchbook from the kitchen counter.
She was laughing. "The rules are that you can't come closer
than ten feet or I'm out of here."

"Sometimes I wonder what desire is. It's a burden, a gift,
and a curse all in one package." I was at the dining room table

fiddling with the sketchbook, writing ART on the first page, then looking up as she quickly shed her clothes.

"You might be a farmer but I bet big money you were an English major in college. I know a bunch of them in Missoula and they always give you that high-minded bullshit when they're trying to get in your pants."

She had me by the gizzard. AD had said that with certain women you're more likely to go all the way if you only talk about spiritual matters or that sort of thing. She was now totally nude and making flowing movements on the living room rug which she said were part of her "tai chi routine," a way of taking advantage of the time during the boredom of posing. I was blinking my eyes, treating them as apertures while I took mental photos for future use. When the November storms hit northern Michigan and I was looking out the window and watching the driven snow slanting sideways across the landscape I could close my eyes and see nude Sylvia. I hadn't seen all that many nude bodies in my life but this was by far the best including magazines. Unfortunately the light in the house was growing dim and I felt dizzy enough to lay my head on the dining room table. I was blacking out because I had forgotten to breathe. She rushed over but my eyes were so blurred I could barely make out her pubis, belly button, and the pink nipples on her apple breasts, McIntosh apples not big Wolf Rivers.

"Jesus Christ, don't die," she shrieked.

"I forgot to breathe." I sucked in air and the room began to resume shape.

Then the phone rang. It actually rang three times in fifteen minutes. I said, "I'm not here" and Sylvia answered,

introducing herself as the "cleaning woman." The first call
was Vivian who insisted a note should be left saying to call
her ASAP. Rather than ruining the mood I liked the can-
did shot of Sylvia on the phone. "I think he got crippled up
from climbing a mountain but he'll be okay."

"Who is Vivian?"

"My ex-wife. She ran off with a guy named Fred last
year and now she sort of wants me back."

"Are you going?" Sylvia scratched her tummy which
gave me a tremor.

"I'm not sure." The phone rang again and this time it
was Robert. Sylvia repeated the mountain climbing injury
story, hung up, and told me to call my son Robert ASAP.
She went back to her tai chi and told me that her mother
had lived with a gambler in Vegas who had been in the top
fifty of the World Series of Poker but he had wanted her to
screw his friends.

"That's too bad," I said. "I bet she's real pretty."

"She's a knockout but she'll crush any man's nuts to
get back to the blackjack table. I'm hungry. Do you mind
frying the fish for me?"

She moved her tai chi to the kitchen while I fried the
fish and made a small salad. The move to the kitchen over-
came the ten-foot barrier and I pinned my dick under my
belt when she turned to answer the phone again. This time
it was Marybelle who wanted me to call her during her lunch
break at 1:00 p.m. California time. It was enervating but I
had to leave the phone plugged in because AD might have
trouble with his flight west.

Her table manners were delightfully messy and when she said, "You know how to fry a fish, kiddo," I glowed. My mom had beaten perfect table manners into me. How many hundreds of times did I hear, "Little Cliff, strong and able, keep your elbows off the table," or "Chew thirty-two times with your mouth closed." Even though the food from your mouth was gone you had to chew thirty-two times.

A droplet of butter from the fried fish had fallen on the upper part of Sylvia's breast and was slowly making its way toward a pink nipple. As Robert would say, "What a visual!" About two-thirds of the way through the meal she glanced up at the wall clock and fairly shouted, "Time's up." She modestly turned her back when she slipped on her clothes and I got the best view yet of her flexed buttocks which would win the Olympics if they had sense enough to have a best butt competition. She hastily finished her meal then lost herself in thought.

"I have to say that a man's dick is the silliest-looking thing in the world. When I was about twelve and doing confession with our priest I asked him why if God wanted us to take men seriously did he give them dicks that look like night crawlers?"

"What did he answer?"

"He said, 'I have no idea, daughter.' Call me if you want another posing session," and then she was out the door and gone with my tightly rolled three one-hundred-dollar bills in her hand. She streaked past the window like a bird of prey. So this is the life of an artist, I mused. I tuned in the NPR station from Bozeman and got a Brahms symphony which was less interesting than nude Sylvia. My brain flitted around like a hummingbird looking for nectar in my last year. Marybelle had been pretty much pure accident, say like a meteorite killing a steer. The only other sexually explosive period of my life had been during the first month of marriage to Viv. Marybelle had come along so late in my life, an absurdly answered prayer, that I thought all too frequently of mere survival.

The phone rang but luckily it was AD who had a three-hour layover in Minneapolis airport and was strictly limiting himself to five drinks. I had given him the number and AD had spoken at length with our fishing guide who had said that thunderstorms were predicted and we might have to go up and fish the Missouri if the Yellowstone got muddy, or perhaps go back to the Big Hole where I had already been if the water wasn't too low. I recognized that AD was just killing time with his cell phone and I wasn't very attentive. I was feeling homesick for northern Michigan, for a home, a farm, that would likely no longer be there in any recognizable condition. I had the idea that they would save the ancient barn because city people think that barns are pretty. Grandpa's place up in the woods would have to suffice though there was a pretty good garden spot.

I was also somewhat dreading certain aspects of AD's visit, not the fishing but the drinking. For more than a decade we had been cooking a bachelor dinner once a month, deciding in advance what subject we would discuss excluding farming and medicine. These dinners didn't start out as bachelor affairs but neither Vivian nor AD's wife at the time found our talk interesting so they went bowling in Petoskey.

AD thought this bowling might be a cover-up for adultery but like most preposterously adulterous men AD was always worried about his wife's faithfulness. Anyway, we tended to drink too much when together. With me it was sometimes a defensive measure because I only got actually drunk when I was with AD who was always discovering new wines for us to try. He tended to drink wine like beer, you know, two sips then down the hatch in big gulps.

I went to my worktable and was soon engrossed in the juvenile book on all the states that I had bought in Bozeman. When I sniffed the air sharply I could still pick up Sylvia's waning scent. After the Brahms they played Mozart's *Jupiter* Symphony which alleviated my stupid melancholy.

MONTANA REDUX VII

I had a bowl of my soothing chicken soup and made my phone calls which turned out to be pleasantly inconsequential. Vivian wanted an address to send contracts and I said I expected to be back home in ten days at which her voice became softer and more cordial. Marybelle only wanted me to check my Dopp kit because she thought she dropped her earrings in there in Nebraska. I found them and she was delighted though when I saw my tube of dick salve at the bottom of the kit it wasn't a sentimental moment. Robert was upset because I had told Vivian that I wouldn't accept his share of the farm. I said that I would put my money in the bank which would give me five grand a year, plus four grand retirement from my years of teaching. I had a place to stay and could heat with wood. I could get farm work or possibly a janitorial job at the school. He said, "Dad, that's seventeen grand below the poverty level. And don't SIGN any contracts with Mom without SHOWING them to a lawyer first. And you have to have health insurance." I didn't tell him that I intended to sell the expensive Tahoe and buy a cheap used pickup which I would need to haul building material to Grandpa's place. I also couldn't explain how much I looked forward to playing the role of my old hero Thoreau in a clearing in the woods. If I visited Bert in midwinter I'd camp out there and back.

On the way to Bozeman I stopped on a mountain pass to watch a gorgeous thunderstorm coming from the south, a regular event up in Michigan but evidently rarer in the west. The guide, Tim, had advised me that the storms might ruin the Yellowstone for a couple of days but I didn't mind getting AD away from the active bar life of Livingston.

At the Bozeman airport the deboarding passengers looked ashen from the bumpy ride and I heard a number say to greeting friends that the plane had been struck by lightning, all the more reason not to get on these tumble-buggies. AD looked especially bad though he was dressed in expensive outdoor clothes as were half the male passengers who had arrived for Montana trout vacations. The word "clones" came to mind at baggage when they picked up their big fly-rod containers with multiple rods. I raised my eyebrows at AD in a mute question.

"Carolyn is filing for divorce because I accidentally gave her herpes. I had a run-in with a biker chick in Kalkaska when I was fishing the Manistee. Carolyn will fleece me. I'll be financially ruined."

I was wondering how you "accidentally" give your wife herpes but didn't say anything. AD always says he's in a state of "financial ruin" for one reason or another but then this would be his third divorce and once again he was culpable. This became even more apparent in the car between Bozeman and Livingston when he admitted he had been treating his wife for what he called "cold sores" and then Carolyn had gone to her mother's doctor on a visit to Chicago and received an accurate diagnosis.

We were driving into the tail end of the thunderstorm which was a nice diversion to someone else's marital woes. AD was "crying in his beer," as we used to say, no more innocent than Hitler, but pretending he was more to be pitied than censured. At age fifty-five AD was finding it hard to be AD. At such times men become the twelve-year-old that dropped the ball in the championship game. "The sun was in my eyes," he yells on a cloudy day.

We stopped at the bar at the Murray Hotel because AD needed a martini for a nightcap and I had nothing at the rental but whiskey and the cases of wine. Tim, our fishing guide, was there, and he said a "slug of mud" was in the river so we should fish the Big Hole for a day and then the Missouri by which time the Yellowstone would be in shape. Way over in the far corner of the bar I could see Sylvia and the masseuse Brandy dancing near the poker machine and suspected the other woman with them to be Sylvia's dreaded mother. AD finished a double Sapphire martini in a trice and ordered another and I went outside with Tim to see if the hitch on the Tahoe would fit his McKenzie boat trailer. He said my friend looked like a cow plot run over by a wagon wheel and I agreed. I mentioned divorce proceedings and he said, "Oh that."

When we got back in the bar AD was half asleep over his second double. Sylvia was just finishing a frenzied dance with Brandy and then came up to the bar for a ginger ale followed by her mother who was attractive indeed but with a trace of glitter in her eyes. We said a polite hello and she bought her mother a Jack Daniel's and coke, an inscrutable drink. I paid for them and Sylvia said, "You're a nice man" which shivered my timbers but I thought how odd to see a girl babysitting her mother and dancing with such passion with her roommate as if no man on earth were suitable. It was at this point that I questioned myself, Cliff, could Sylvia be a daughter of Sappho? Very likely.

I felt lucky that AD was comatose enough not to notice Sylvia and her mother which normally would have set him off like a Fourth of July rocket. Dad used to say "thank god for small favors" when a whole litter of piglets survived. The memory of bottle feeding a piglet made me homesick. I half carried AD to his bedroom where he collapsed fully dressed, then precooked some spuds and put out sausage to thaw for breakfast.

Tim arrived at 6:00 a.m., and AD was in fairly good shape eating what he also called a "heart stopper" breakfast. We reached the Big Hole in two and a half hours and fished until dinnertime at the Hitch'n Post where AD chugged a bottle of "despicable" California wine and was asleep at eight in the evening. What saved us from larger considerations like life herself was the exhaustion of dragging the boat at times when the water was low, the heat and stinging yellow jackets, and the fishing itself because there was a hatch of spruce moths and fish were rising everywhere. AD smelled

like he was sweating pure gin and only became problemati-
cal at lunch on the riverbank when he delivered a manic
rehash of his three marriages. For a change he didn't play
himself as the insulted and the injured, in fact concluded by
saying, "I won every argument and I was always wrong."
AD is a fierce and eloquent debater and I could see how that
was possible. AD insisted that it was our hopeless and antic
glandular fevers that led us astray. He said, "Some men will
climb the same mountain hundreds of times while other men
need to climb hundreds of mountains." Tim, who had also
been married three times, said his wandering had only been
a search for the "right one" but AD said that was bullshit
because who we think of as the right one could change every
week or so and that maybe it was the craziness of the sexual
impulse that kept the world populated. They continued wrangling and I clambered up the bank to the railroad tracks that
ran along the river on the other side of which was a marsh
and a spring-fed pool containing a few large trout, clearly
trapped there. I had had a pretty bourgeois life because
farmers haven't the time or many opportunities to chase
stray ladies. AD and Tim had lived a river life and I was more
like the fish trapped in the spring pool except maybe they
didn't know they were trapped in a spring pool.

We left at dawn driving north to the Missouri River
near Cascade south of Great Falls. It was cool enough when
we arrived but by noon the temperature was already in the
low nineties and we ran out of drinking water a full two
hours before we reached the site where we could get off the
river. AD stupidly poured one bottle of drinking water over
his head then lamely apologized. Neither trout nor fisher-

men like this kind of heat so the day was a blowout. The Missouri in this area is like a hundred-yard-wide, crystal-line spring creek, truly beautiful, but was quite weedy from the prolonged heat wave. I leaned over the gunnel and stared at many large trout we passed over who, sensibly enough, seemed to be snoozing. We intercepted a large bull snake about six feet long as it crossed the river and were amazed that the snake attacked the boat. Tim said that bull snakes kill and eat rattlers.

We felt like roadkill driving to our motel in Great Falls even after sharing a gallon of water from a convenience store. AD was half asleep in the backseat nursing at a bottle of hot vodka from his luggage. We only picked at bad steaks for dinner and AD drank a procession of doubles. We stopped at a strip club and AD was smitten by a lovely heavily freckled stripper and stood up bellowing the words to the song, "My heart cries for you." He wouldn't stop so the biker-type bouncers threw him out. He wept on the way back to the motel and we had to half carry him to his room. I was concerned but Tim said, "Don't worry about the asshole. He's a big boy."

At dawn we drove four hours east just past Livingston to Big Timber and had about five hours of miraculous brown-trout fishing and also saw seven golden eagles and nine bald. Much of the time AD was asleep in the back of the boat so missed nearly everything.

The final disaster struck in the evening during a splen-did meal at the Bistro. AD had apparently taken a pep pill as some doctors do and had sidled up to the bar and had a drink with Sylvia's mother and Brandy the masseuse. When

Sylvia served me a piece of chocolate cake and took away
AD's uneaten meal she asked about him. I reassured her
without confidence that AD was a doctor friend from northern Michigan which seemed to allay her fears but when I
came out of the toilet they had vanished. I checked the
Murray bar and they weren't there so I went back to the
rental and had a good night's sleep.

At seven in the morning Sylvia ran out in tears to tell
me that Brandy had called from Bozeman to say that AD
and Sylvia's mother had caught the early plane to Salt Lake
headed for Las Vegas. I was dumbfounded but counseled
Sylvia that it was time for her to stop looking after her mother.
I cooked her an omelet and halfway through eating it she
decided to agree with me. I gave her a ride back to her apartment and she kissed me on the cheek which gave me a de-
layed shudder. I had two more fine days fishing with Tim
and then packed for home without a phone call from AD.
Sylvia had the night off and came out the last evening for
my patented spaghetti and meatball recipe of which she ate
a great deal. We played double solitaire for a while and
watched *L.A. Law*. I very much wanted to ask her for another
posing session for the health of my project but it seemed
inappropriate. She sensed the depth of my melancholy and
gave me an electrifying thirty-second "freebie," lifting her
blouse and dropping her shorts and doing a little twirl.
Tears formed because I doubted I would ever see her again.
I walked her home as far as the Ninth Street Bridge and we
paused to look down at the sweet-smelling, turbulent river.
I said, "Life is a river," and she said, "No, a river is a river
and life is life." I felt corrected.

MICHIGAN

I made tracks as we used to say, leaving brown trout and
Sylvia in my past. I didn't even stop to look at cows. I fled
Livingston at dawn like a refugee fleeing a war-torn country, or maybe not, maybe just a geezer heading home. Near
Miles City I talked to Robert for five minutes and then an
OnStar voice said I had run out of time, adding instructions
on how to buy more time with a credit card. I think the voice
came from New Jersey. Robert was absolutely jolly at the
idea that his dad was heading home to see his mom, and I
certainly wasn't going to correct him by saying that my
motive was to fix up Grandpa's place in order to have the
necessary solitude for my literary project which I had mentally enmeshed in the larger world of art. To be sure, I was
at the bottom of the barrel but who knows what the future
will bring? I had written a few haiku in college that my literary friends thought were awful. Here is my favorite:

I want to look at a cow
without my mind saying "cow."

I reached Jamestown in twelve hours, had a brisket sandwich, then laid out my project work on my motel desk. Due to the fatigue of driving I was without insights. I was back at the desk before dawn having used two bags in the coffeemaker which only made me a wide-awake fantasist with the visual of Sylvia's butt drifting across the blank page. Did this mean biology was stronger than art? Probably.

I made Iron Mountain in the gathering dark after fifteen hours of driving. I went to Vantana's, a restaurant I'd heard about, and had the special called "The Italian Holiday" which was Italian sausage, a huge meatball, spaghetti, and gnocchi, all covered with marinara. This virtual mound of nutrition put me to sleep pronto.

Up at dawn again I reached Vivian's real estate office just as her snotty secretary was leaving for lunch. This young woman had a peculiar accent of her own devising and could look at me without seeing me. She pointed at Viv's closed door and said a "closing" was in process. I fell asleep on a plush sofa reading a *National Geographic* article called "Uzbekistan Faces the Future." The future, as always, turned out to be uncertain.

"Cliff, you look like a turd struck with a meat ax," Viv said loudly, waking me with a start. She was pretty trim in a blue suit though her new hairdo was mounded higher than my last night's Italian meal.

She went to the window and waved at the departing clients in their silver Mercedes.

"These folks bought five Petoskey condos on spec. My commission will be a cool hundred grand," she crowed. I reflected that this amount was my net worth not counting my Tahoe.

On the way to Petoskey for lunch Viv gave me the startling news that she had bailed AD out of a mess in Las Vegas. He had tapped out his credit card gambling and a "whore" he was with had beaten on a slot machine with a high heel doing real damage. Viv had bailed them out of the slammer because she thought it wasn't proper for a doctor to be in jail.

At the Chinese restaurant in Petoskey Viv said, "We grew in different directions" which seemed to me a unique description of her fling with Fred. Viv tore into a beef and vegetable stir-fry rattling on about the subtleties of her low-carb diabetic diet. Frankly, she looked better than she had in ten years and my mind whirled at the thought of her thousands of powdered donuts and Pepsis (when I took her returnable deposit cans to the store I got to keep half the money). She had two tablespoons of my white rice and squeezed her eyes shut with pleasure after which she stared at our Chinese waiter and asked, "Is it true Chinese men have small weenies?" I answered that maybe there was a weenie Web site she could find on her computer and she said, "Probably."

After lunch she drove me to her house which was rather lavish but she said she had got a real deal bidding in a bank-ruptcy sale. All the rooms were carpeted in white except the kitchen and all the furniture and walls were also white. I started sneezing wildly from the wooly perfumed smell.

"This house will never smell like cow shit and it's strictly no smoking, kiddo."

I took a nap on the screened front porch while she went back to work for an hour or so. I reflected that I had driven like a maniac for this questionable welcome. I dozed intermittently, fearful of the upcoming trip over to the farm which she was insisting on so I could "face reality." I glanced through the glass doors of the porch at the house's white interior, definitely my least favorite color. Once again my antic neurons gave me a glance of Sylvia's pubis. I mused on the accidental nature of the sexual contacts of my life. Babe at the diner when we were both mischievously lonely, then the haphazard typhoon of Marybelle, a climatic accident. And way back when with Vivian who acted like she was in great demand which I even doubted at the time. She was a true American girl, a little loud and boisterous, a 4-H girl whose heifer had won at the county fair, a straight C student who only pretended she read the books I gave her, but all and all likable, and there also was the idea that I had no frame of reference to talk smoothly with the few city girls I dated.

We drove over to our old farm and I wept like a baby stung by a bee. My attached shed was gone and the barn was painted bright red. The orchard had been bulldozed and seeded and surrounded by white board fences à la Kentucky. The house had been razed and an enormous brick dwelling was being built in its place and where the chicken coop had been there was a brick stable with seven box stall doors with horses looking out and at least fifty workmen bustling around the place. We drove on down the road and stopped by a marsh where Viv embraced me and patted my back as if I were a baby needing to be burped.

"They're putting a couple of mil into that place," she said.

"I hope maggots eat their brains." I was still sniffling.

"That's unlikely what with embalming fluid. When the going gets tough, the tough get doing. Now that you've seen the raw meat on the floor you have to start a new life at your grandpa's place."

I dropped Viv off at her house because she was making us a candlelit fried chicken dinner. I headed toward Grandpa's thinking about a work schedule for my project but also thinking about stopping at the humane society dog pound to pick up a pup. Of course writers and other artists have varied work habits but I thought I remembered that Thoreau chose early morning after a stroll. Not a day had passed in the four months since Lola had died that I didn't think of getting another dog as I hadn't been without one since college. It was anyway certain that I wouldn't be able to bring a dog into Viv's new place. Robert had said with a laugh that Viv was hanging out with "the movers and shakers" in the area whoever they were and I would steadfastly avoid them.

Seeing a traffic jam up ahead in the road along Walloon Lake I made a quick detour. It was obvious what had happened. There were two ambulances on shore and a flotilla of boats out front with two big water ski boats in bad shape from a collision. Bert and I used to do orchard work on a farm up the road and at lunch break we'd sit on the hillside and watch the rich kids zipping up and down the lake. When there was an accident Bert would say, "Maybe another dummy out of the gene pool."

I didn't spend much time at Grandpa's but my heart swelled with pleasure at living in this remote place, a forty-acre bushy pasture forming a clearing in the dense hilly woods, a perfect place for my art. Viv had thought the Indian's shabby hut to be unlivable and had sent some workmen over to get the kitchen ready and organize a makeshift sleeping quarters in the small dining room. The back two bedrooms were pretty much burned down and were separated from the dining room with tacked-up Visqueen plastic. I'd have to see if there was a way to get the burned odor out of the air. All in all I felt suddenly damned fine about my prospects. Out front there was still a rope hanging from a maple limb that used to hold a tire swing Grandpa and my dad had built for me and Teddy. I unloaded my stuff, including the jigsaw puzzle which I put on the Formica kitchen table that was a nice shade of yellow. Viv had put a six-pack in the fridge and I toasted to my new life with a can of beer. There was also a stack of frozen diet dinners in the fridge's freezer compartment which a new dog might enjoy.

On the way home I stopped by the dog pound just as it was closing for the day. I was drawn to a pup that was a collie-shepherd cross but then it was sitting there with its shaggy old mother and I wondered if I had the craw to separate them. Chances are the mother would quickly end her life in the gas chamber. On the way down the road I was pulled this way and that by the mother and pup and by the time I reached Viv's I could see I'd have to take both. After all, the mother would help babysit the pup and maybe the attractive young woman attendant at the dog pound would become well disposed to me. She filled out her Levi's and T-shirt real nice and maybe she would come out for a visit. And so on with the fantasy so that I nearly hit one of Viv's pink flamingo lawn ornaments when I pulled into her drive.

The fried chicken was fine indeed though I was put off by the patchouli odor of the scented candles. When I came up to the back steps I could hear the music from *Kismet* but she was kind enough to turn it off. There were no mashed potatoes and chicken gravy because Viv said she couldn't bear to see me eat them when they were forbidden to her. She drank a glass of vodka with lemon because it was "low sugar."

After dinner we sat out front on a porch swing, about the only piece of furniture she saved from our old home. She showed me some diabetes diet cookbooks and suggested that I should come over once a week and cook her dinner but I would have to adapt the recipes. My pot roast with onions or rutabaga but no potatoes. Mexican chili with no beans, spaghetti and meatballs with no spaghetti. I was agreeable partly because I was drinking a large glass of vodka having pushed aside a syrupy California wine that had cost her seven bucks. I impulsively slid a hand down her blouse and felt one of her large tits. She blushed and glowed but pushed my hand away saying we might work into it as time passed. She tweaked my trousers and said, "I think it's cute that your dick still gets hard for me, Cliff."

She got up to make me a sobering cup of instant coffee and while she was away I thought how nice it would be to go to Guatemala with Sylvia and work in an orphanage but that was as unlikely as peace on earth. I needed to buy dog dishes and food, a crowbar and hammer, a scythe to cut the weeds around Grandpa's house, sell the Tahoe and buy a used pickup. Dawn would find me at my kitchen table making decisions on renaming the states, and then setting up a bird feeder. I shook Viv's big soft hand and drove home in the summer twilight with a mellow heart.

I was up at first light with a trace of dawn visible through the east kitchen window. I drank half of my coffee on the rickety back porch most of the floorboards of which I'd have to replace. I set off for a stroll with an imaginary dog at my side, my trousers soon wet to the knees with dew. I saw an indigo bunting flitting around a dogwood bush, possibly a bird name not to be changed. I seem to be with the mute Indian inspecting a fox burrow in the southwest corner of the pasture. A Jersey milk cow is following us. I look back at the bungalow which is catching the light of the orange rising sun. Grandpa is drinking his coffee with a splash of Four Roses whiskey for his heart. Teddy sits in a puddle in the driveway. Dad is digging earthworms in the corner of the yard so we can catch bluegills to fry up for lunch. And here I am fifty years later, an old body bent on a new life.

APPENDIX

I've been home for a month and things have been up and down which apparently is the nature of life, at least on earth. I get up at 4:00 a.m. and work on my new calling until about eight and then proceed with the house remodeling. The scent of the fire is still there but I'm getting used to it in the same way that we learn to accept widespread political malfeasance. I checked the Richardson biography out of the Harbor Springs library and was quite startled to discover that Ralph Waldo Emerson was emotionally a much livelier fellow than he presents himself in his austere essays.

I've only been seeing Viv once a week but she has definitely been a cross to bear. She can't stop fibbing to herself and me. I cooked her a dinner of diet fajitas the other evening and when I went to the toilet to pee she definitely put a chunk of butter in the pan with the onions, peppers, and beef. Later when I took out the garbage at her request I noted illegal (for her diabetes) empty packages of English muffins and Oreos. At least there was no sign of powdered donuts or Pepsi.

Lothar has been quite a problem. Though the original Lothar was a male I gave the name to the female pup because she was beige colored and strong. My favorite Sunday morning comic strip as a kid was *Mandrake the Magician*. Mandrake's beautiful wife was named Narda and his powerful Afro-American henchman who was invincible was named Lothar. Lothar was my first hero and I wanted to be a huge strong black man when I grew up. Dad was patient in explaining to me that this wasn't possible. He himself wanted to be Charlie Chan but we couldn't change our colors any more than a Holstein cow could become a Guernsey. This was a harsh lesson. All of us starlings can't become ospreys.

Lothar has developed the unfortunate habit of flopping on the floor and sinking her teeth in my pant cuff so that I have to drag her around the kitchen floor when I make my morning coffee. Oddly enough she detaches her teeth when I pour my first cup at which point I let her out to pee. She yaps furiously at the outside world and pees on the porch. As I've said I've been getting up in the dark at 4:00 a.m. to work on my art. Tragedy struck little Lothar a scant week after I brought she and her mother home from the dog pound. I named the mother after my mother's cousin Edna who was also extraordinarily top heavy on her spindly little legs. After a few days with us Edna the dog developed a severe salivary gland infection which required surgery and five trips to the vet before her lungs filled with fluid and she became a heavy dog corpse. I kept Lothar in the car while I buried her mom behind the Indian's shack. The total bill from the vet was $2,700, close to the amount spent on my trip west. Vets have become as expensive as human doctors. I thought I should stop at the dog pound and tell them of Edna's passing. The pretty young woman seemed totally unconcerned, saying, "Win some, lose some." She was doing one of those number puzzles called sudoku and didn't meet my glance. She was still wearing the attractive trousers that pulled up tightly in her pubis and I had simultaneous thoughts of sex and dog death.

The next evening when I cooked meat loaf and succotash for Viv at her request, I told her the dog story including the cost and she said, "Poor Cliff and his mutts," as if I were a third person. She stuffed a greenback in my front pocket to help with the bill. She was distracted by a pending sale of a beach house in Harbor Springs for two million and furious that her commission had been negotiated down to fifty thousand. It was hard to be sympathetic. Evidently real estate was the contemporary Lost Dutchman mine only it was found. On the way home I checked Viv's gift and it was a twenty, not much of a dent in my vet mud bath.

A few days later I let out a victory cry from the porch at dawn when I finished renaming our fifty states. Even as a neophyte I felt that tingling epiphany shared by many in the history of the arts. I was humble but this was a far cry from Marybelle's verbal abuse about the project in Wyoming or Sylvia jokingly tossing me a teeny-weeny pad to sketch her body. Thoughts of Sylvia's bare butt were sullying my exalted art thoughts so I took Lothar for a stroll around the forty acres. I saw an indigo bunting, a possible good omen, and then Lothar was bitten on the nose by a now rare blue racer snake. This was likely a coincidence. I mean the sky was also blue so how far can I go with the shades of blue in a bird or a snake? Lothar squealed from her nose bite and circled around the snake for a new angle of attack. She was furious when I grabbed her and hauled her away. Luckily she plays so hard for brief periods that her naps are very long.

It was one of the better days of my life. I worked hard all morning, and for lunch shared some celebratory pork steak with Lothar who aggressively rends the meat with her baby teeth. After a fine nap I took Lothar for a long walk in order to exhaust her so I could go back to my remodeling without her playful intervention. During our walk a wasp bit her and she chased it to exhaustion. I left a spade back by a seep near a tiny creek in hopes of uncovering a spring for a bathing hole. I have given up trying to stop Lothar from eating the worms in my spadefuls of dirt or the little frogs she jumps in the creek. It's certain that she is never going to be a pretty girl what with her overlarge head and shoulders. The vet had guessed that her mother might have been a Lab and bulldog mix but Lothar's father was probably a larger mongrel. By evening I was quite tired and gave up the idea of driving to town for a few drinks and a look at the Saturday night ladies. Everyone knows the country roads are dangerous on Saturday night with the rich summer riffraff swerving around at high speed in their expensive cars. Instead I had chicken soup in which I had chopped too many jalapeños and discovered again that a stiff single drink on the porch on a summer evening can be like going to the church of your "self."

In my twilight bedtime I looked at my card-table desk with pride, the stacks of books and papers that they called "research tools" back at Michigan State University. And there in a cleared area was my list of the states and their new names, not that the states were gleaming in the gathering dark. I thought perhaps I should try to find an actual type-writer at a yard sale. I certainly wasn't going to get suckered in on the computer craze and the shit storm of e-mails people eat up their time with. I knew that an artist must stand alone off to the side of contemporary fashion.

Unfortunately I was to discover that renaming the birds of North America was a much more volatile project. I joined a small group of bird-watchers very early one morning only to discover that the arts can be a cruel mistress indeed. I had seen on the post office bulletin board a notice of a meeting of a birding group and decided to go in hopes of meeting an amiable woman. I showed up at the Round Lake Preserve, a Nature Conservancy property, at 5:30 a.m. There were a half dozen women in the parking lot, all of them older than me except for a retired teacher of Spanish from Detroit who attached herself to me like a decal. She was in her midfifties, named Mara, and had the unfortunate habit of sprinkling her monologues with Spanish phrases so that I never knew what she was talking about. The ladies all wore the rather eccentric sporting garb of birders and I felt shabby with my cheap binoculars. We tromped around for an hour with the birding uneventful because most species were quiet during early August molting. I announced that I had seen a yellow warbler, but as a newcomer to the group it was apparent that I lacked credibility.

The hideous denouement occurred on the dock where we were all glassing a distant mother loon and her two nearly grown chicks. By this time everyone was pretty friendly and I was enjoying a vague feeling of desirability. The only untoward event had been when Mara had stepped near a large garter snake, then screeched and clutched at me in fear. My hand had inadvertently touched her breast and she leapt back giving me a cold stare as if I had done it on purpose. I couldn't think of anything to say. Anyway, we were out on the dock and they were all behind me and I stupidly began rattling on about my art project of renaming the birds of North America. I recited a couple of dozen of my name changes including the "banker bird" for the nuthatch because it saves so many more seeds than it can eat, the "beige dolorosa" for the brown thrasher, the "Rubens" for the robin, and so on. Far out on the lake the loon gave her lovely quavering call and I paused in my speech hearing a squeaky, keening sound behind me. I turned and all six of them had a look of horror as if they had found themselves standing in a sandbox chock-full of dog shit. Norma, their leader, swung her hawthorn cane narrowly missing my nose. I stepped back barely saving myself from falling off the end of the dock. They hurled epithets at me like "pig," "fool," "you're disgusting," then turned and marched off the dock like storm troopers. It was certainly obvious that they didn't want me to change the names of the birds of North America.

On the drive home I recalled James Joyce's motto "Silence, exile, cunning," and resolved to adopt it as my own. I also remembered a musical appreciation lecture as a freshman in college where the professor had said the great Stravinsky had been roundly booed at the first performance of *The Firebird* in Paris.

Even Lothar was furious at me when I let her out of the Indian's shack though I quickly reentered her good graces by giving her a portion of leftover pot roast and gravy. Would that all females were this easy but then Lothar had a fat gnarled face like a brown frog and wasn't much of a challenge. I glanced over at the card table and wondered what problems my renamed states might cause but then it was unlikely that the changes would become widely known. It was probably better to be a flower born to blush unseen in the desert air as some English poet had said.

I took Lothar for a midmorning walk in the gathering heat packing along a small flask of schnapps to calm my nerves which were improbably frayed. It had been my dad's flask which he kept full for what he called "emergencies." About a quarter mile out I heard a car on the gravel road and instinctively ducked down behind a clump of thornapple bushes. I still had my bird-watching binoculars and glassed Vivian as she went through the house and out on the back porch where she hollered "Cliff! Cliff! Cliff! I have papers for you to sign!" I knelt there behind the bushes thinking that she would always have papers for me to sign.

She finally drove away and I proceeded on to the spring with Lothar beating me there and muddying up the water in a frantic search for a frog to eat. I took off my clothes and sat down in the cool water, sipping at my schnapps and looking up at the way the sun dappled down through the beech and sugar-maple leaves. This won't be a bad life I thought happily. What there is left of it is undetermined but I'll do fine.

The Renamed States

Alabama – Chickasaw	Nebraska – Poncapawnee
Alaska – Koyukon	Nevada – Paiute
Arizona – Apache	New Hampshire – Wappinger
Arkansas – Caddo	
California – Chumash	New Jersey – Nakyssan
Colorado – Ute	New Mexico – Navajo
Connecticut – Mohegan	New York – Iroquois
Delaware – Nanticoke	North Carolina – Shawnee
Florida – Seminole	North Dakota – Hidatsa
Georgia – Creek	Ohio – Wyandot
Hawaii – Kanaka Maoli	Oklahoma – Cherokee
Idaho – Nez Perce	Oregon – Umatilla
Illinois – Kickapoo	Pennsylvania – Onondaga
Indiana – Plankeshaw	Rhode Island – Wampanoag
Iowa – Foxsauk	South Carolina – Catawba
Kansas – Wichita	South Dakota – Lakota
Kentucky – Wea	Tennessee – Yuchi
Louisiana – Acolapissa	Texas – Comanche
Maine – Abnaki	Utah – Ute
Maryland – Powhatan	Vermont – Pequot
Massachusetts – Paugusett	Virginia – Santee
Michigan – Potawatomi	Washington – Tilamook
Minnesota – Ojibway	West Virginia – Catawba
Mississippi – Choctaw	Wisconsin – Menominee
Missouri – Osage	Wyoming – Cheyenne
Montana – Absaroka	

SEP - - 2008

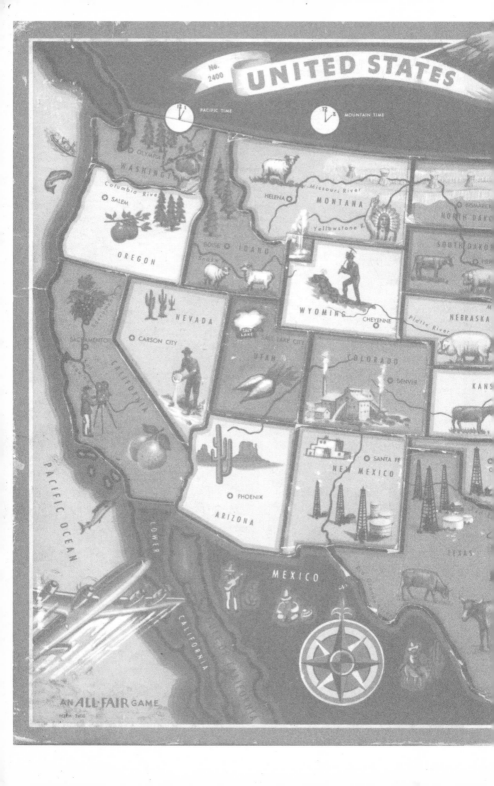